The BINDING

Salma is the pen name of Rajathi, is one of the most significant and courageous voices of contemporary Tamil literature. A poet, novelist and activist, she has forged a unique path by transforming the cloistered reality of her life into powerful art that has universal appeal and challenges the deeply entrenched social and patriarchal norms, particularly within the Tamil Muslim community.

Salma's literary career is marked by several seminal works that have earned her critical acclaim and a devoted following. She is the author of several poetry collections such as *Oru Maalaiyum Innoru Maalaiyum* (*One Evening and Another Evening*) and *Pachchai Devathai* (*Green Angel*); short story collections *Saabam, Balyam and Curse*; and novels *Irandaam Jaamangalin Kadhai* (*The Dark Hours of the Night*) (2025) and *Manamiyangal* (*Women Dreaming*) (2020). *Adaikkum Thaazh* (*The Binding*) is her third novel.

In 2001, Salma was elected as the Panchayat President of Ponnampatti in the Tiruchirappalli district. She was later appointed as the Chairperson of the Tamil Nadu Social Welfare Board (2006–2011) and was instrumental in launching several welfare schemes, including landmark initiatives for the transgender community. An active member of the Dravida Munnetra Kazhagam (DMK), she has served in various party roles, including Deputy Secretary of the Women's Wing. In 2025, Salma was nominated as a Member of Parliament, Rajya Sabha.

Janani Kannan is a US-based interior architect who enjoys translating Tamil novels and short stories into English. Her translation of Perumal Murugan's novel *Fire Bird* received the 2023 JCB Prize for Literature and was shortlisted for the Crossword Popular Choice Award 2024. Her published translations of short stories include the works of contemporary Tamil writers, such as Imayam, Latha, Vannanilayan, Su. Ra., Shobashakti and Sujatha Selvaraj.

Originally from Chennai, Janani rediscovered her love for all things Tamil as a young adult. Her self-professed anthropological interests also include collecting and chronicling anecdotes, recipes and architectural nuggets from Tamil culture.

The BINDING

SALMA

Translated by

JANANI KANNAN

MACMILLAN

First published 2025 by Macmillan
an imprint of Pan Macmillan Publishing India Private Limited
707 Kailash Building
26 K. G. Marg, New Delhi 110001
www.panmacmillan.co.in

Pan Macmillan, The Smithson, 6 Briset Street, Farringdon, London EC1M 5NR
Associated companies throughout the world
www.panmacmillan.com

ISBN 978-93-6113-950-5

1 3 5 7 9 8 6 4 2

Typeset in ITC Galliard Pro by R. Ajith Kumar, New Delhi
Printed and bound in India by Thomson Press India Ltd.

To my beloved granddaughter
Smaya Saleem

Translator's Note

To Anu Joni Bala

Anbirkkum undoe adaikkunthaazh Aarvalar
Pun-kaneer poosal tharum

– Ambudaimai, Kural 71,
Thirukkural by THIRUVALLUVAR

Can there be aught of bolt that bars the doors of love?
O, nay!
The drops of tears of loving ones will soon that love betray!

– Translation by 'THIRUVACHAKAMANI'
K. M. BALASUBRAMANIAM

In this compelling novel, Salma traces the life of Rasangam, a young man growing up in a remote rural hamlet in Tamil Nadu, who is bound by orthodox Muslim family values and beliefs. The narrative follows his struggle as he finds himself in a restrictive and judgmental society that forces him to question his identity and reshape his perceptions. Salma delicately unveils Rasangam's desires, insecurities and inner conflicts to reveal how his choices reverberate through the lives of his siblings and extended family once he inevitably assumes the role of the patriarch.

The original Tamil novel, the author's third, was published in 2022. It borrows its title *Adaikkum Thaazh* from the *Thirukkural*, and roughly translates to 'The Binding Latch', outside the context of the source couplet. It is apt for a novel so deeply concerned with the perilous nature of love, especially in interfaith relationships, exposing the constraints and moral boundaries around love in the name of social order. Salma brings the story full circle by extending the narrative to the next generation through Imran, Rasangam's son, juxtaposing evolving modern struggles against enduring social prejudices.

Salma draws extensively on her own experience of growing up under the overbearing constraints typical of conservative religious families to bring rich detail and realism to her narrative. Her tendency to question and confront the treatment of women in such societies emerges through the subtle misogynistic nuances and the implicit hierarchies she peppers throughout the story. At some level, there seems to be a direct parallel between the structure of the novel and lived experience: although the story is centred on a patriarch and his son, the female characters in their lives are portrayed as displaying great emotional and psychological depth and resilience.

Reading this book felt – to borrow a cliché – like skinning an onion. Initially, I was absorbed by the character of Rasangam and the story itself. Then, as I delved into it further, I found myself drawn to the secondary characters, like Hanifa, Fathima, Rasiya and Anitha, each of whom lingered in my thoughts long after I had closed the book. Alongside the characters is a wealth of cultural context that deeply satisfied my appetite for anthropological minutiae. Having grown up in a Hindu family and attended a Catholic school, I am broadly familiar with Hindu and Christian practices, but it dawned on me only after reading this book how little I knew about the Tamil Muslim community.

This realization also informed my approach to translating Salma's Tamil, enriched with Arabic words and expressions naturalized into Tamil, that posed both a challenge and an opportunity for learning. I often had to trace the Tamilized forms back to their Arabic roots to understand the nuance and usage. Naturally, this has deepened my appreciation for the Tamil language for its ability to fold history into its layers.

Aside from the challenges of translating one language into another, this novel posed the additional challenge of remaining true to the novel's regional and communal contexts and conveying those to the reader as well. Doing my best to remain true to the spirit of the original work, I often fought my urge to over-annotate. I am indebted to Kalyan Raman for sharing his valuable insights into the art of translation, both through lively conversations and his review of a slice of this work.

This project is particularly special to me as it arrived at the time when I had chosen to take a break from my professional life as an interior architect. Not only did it give me a renewed sense of purpose, it also helped me find focus and start living by some of the life lessons I'd only ever read about before. I am very grateful to Kannan Sundaram from Kalachuvadu, once again, for entrusting me with this opportunity.

It has been nothing short of inspiring knowing the ever-cheerful Salma. We connected instantly during our first meeting in Chennai and she has continued to remain warm, approachable and available to me, despite her recent appointment as a Rajya Sabha Member of Parliament from Tamil Nadu.

My heartfelt thanks to Pujitha Krishnan, Udyotna Kumar and the rest of the Pan Macmillan India team for their editorial support as well as the beautiful cover design and title. There is an undeniable joy in working alongside talented, perceptive women!

As always, none of this would have been possible without the unwavering support of my family. My husband kindly forgot about me for a few weeks and my ten-year-old felt proud reading and helping his amma edit her work, honing his own language skills along the way.

And finally, to Chennai – the city and my people here – thank you for welcoming me with open arms and for giving me countless reasons to feel alive.

Janani Kannan
November 2025
Chennai

1

Village 1

STANDING KNEE-DEEP IN THE CHANNEL, AJMAL PUT HIS hand inside a burrow on the bank and quickly pulled out the crab he had caught.

'*Dei*, it's going to bite you!' Aabida shrieked, rapping him lightly on his shaven head.

'Go away, akka,' he said as he gently put the baby crab into his tiffin box and closed the lid tight.

The sky was growing dark; a lightning bolt flickered above the distant horizon. Settling down on the branch of a young portia tree that she had climbed effortlessly, Aabida opened the drawstring pouch at her hip and reached for the anjarepetti murukku inside. It had crumbled to bits. 'It's broken ...' she groaned in dismay. 'Oh well, who cares!' she exclaimed, scooping out the powdery fragments of the rose cookie and pouring them into her mouth. Relishing its crunchiness, she let her legs dangle in the air and began to swing them back and forth.

'You'll get walloped if you don't stop swinging

your legs … Behaving like a boy!' her mother's voice frightened Aabida. She immediately stopped moving her legs and looked at her mother.

Sainambu shook out the free end of her voile sari and prepared to return home. 'I am leaving, you should leave too,' she said to Picchaimani, who was cleaning his short-handled hoe in the channel's running water. Her round, reddened face was stern.

'Okay, amma,' he responded.

She reached for the drawstring purse knotted into the free end of her sari and handed him some money. 'Now go and buy the groceries before it gets dark. Looks like it's about to rain, too,' she said with concern. 'Come, children, let's go home,' she said aloud.

Hearing his mother's high-pitched voice, Ajmal hastily opened his tiffin box to check on the crab one more time, closed the lid and got ready to leave. He clutched his shorts, which were slipping from his waist.

'Picchaimani, I can't climb down – can you please give me a hand?' Aabida whined.

'Donkey of a girl! You knew how to climb up, but you don't know how to climb down? Straighten your skirt, you wretch!' scowled Sainambu. 'Picchaimani, help her down.'

'Let it go, amma, don't scold the child,' Picchaimani said, reaching out his arms to help Aabida.

Wrapping the portia flowers and fruits in the free end of her half-sari and tucking it at her waist, Aabida raced past her mother. Ajmal followed, gripping his ill-fitting shorts with one hand and his tiffin box with the other.

Large raindrops began falling on the ground. The children continued running while Sainambu walked with an umbrella in her hand. She called out loudly after them, 'Don't run! Walk under the umbrella, children!' But the kids raced on ahead, paying no heed. Their mother's voice was scattered by the howling winds and rain.

2

AS THE BELLOWING SMOKE RISING FROM THE EARTHEN stove stung Fathima's eyes, tears rolled down her face. She poured batter onto the griddle to make a *dosai* and huffed through the blow-pipe, coaxing the reluctant embers under the stove to ignite. *Getting this green coconut husk to burn will be the death of me*, she thought. '*Saniyan* ...' she cursed aloud and continued to blow until a feeble fire began to sputter as if out of pity for her.

Twelve, she counted mentally before saying it aloud and adding it to the stack on a plate beside her.

Muqdhar Maamu and Jagir Nanna were sitting on the front pyol.

'How many dosais are here?' Sainambu asked as she came into the kitchen and picked up the plate.

'Twelve,' Fathima replied curtly.

'Giving me attitude, are you? Watch it or I will thrash you!' she hissed at her niece, took the plate of dosais to the two men outside, divided the dosais equally between them and said, 'Please eat'. Carrying the empty plate back into the kitchen, she flung it across the floor towards

Fathima. 'Make more dosais,' she ordered and returned to serve sambhar on the guests' plates.

Fathima mumbled inaudibly as she wiped away her smoke-induced tears. The pile of dosais on the plate began growing once again. She dragged the end of her voile sari across her sweaty face.

'Akka, I'm hungry, give me some dosais,' Rasangam said as he entered the kitchen and grabbed a palmyra mat to sit down next to his cousin. 'My eyes are getting teary – isn't there a lot of smoke in here?'

'All thanks to your mother, *da*. Look at her, announcing to all and sundry on the street that we are making dosais at home and bringing them home to be fed. Meanwhile, it is my eyes that burn from the smoke,' Fathima complained.

'Never mind, they are our relatives, after all. You know it's only because they don't make any in their own homes. Besides, amma is always this way,' Rasangam consoled his elder cousin. 'But even in the middle of this thick cloud of smoke, you're glowing like Jayalalitha, akka!' he teased, just to provoke her.

'You are such a … Anyway, I can't give you any dosais right now – go away. Let those two finish eating first. My hands ache badly from grinding the batter and pouring out so many dosais.'

'Don't worry, akka, if your hands become stiff with pain, we can loosen them with salve,' Rasangam teased.

'Make me some too, I'll be right back.' He went into the front yard and called out, 'Dei Ajmal! Aabida! Where are you?'

'I'm here!' Ajmal shouted in the direction of the courtyard, leaning out from the terrace.

'Come, let's eat,' Rasangam called to them and then walked over to Hanifa annan, whom he spotted lying on a rope cot inside the house. 'Do I have to invite you separately? Come, let's eat.'

'I'm not hungry,' Hanifa replied, sitting up.

Ever since Attha died, all he does is lie on the cot and stare blankly at the ceiling, Rasangam thought. Remembering his father always filled him with sadness. His mind refused to acknowledge that he was no more and was never going to return.

His father, Anwar, used to regularly travel to Singapore for trade from a very young age and had transformed into quite the man of culture. From various household appliances to the latest shoes and handbags, he was the first one to introduce their tiny hamlet to all such things, which he would bring back for his wife, Sainambu, and his younger brother's wife, Mahamooda.

Indeed, no one could forget him. Amma had been completely crushed when he died. It was only over the last few months since the Iddah period ended that she had begun to return to – to an extent – her usual self. There was not a household in their village that didn't have the Axe Brand pain-relief oil that he gave out generously.

He kept a suitcase full of them at home and handed a bottle to anyone he met. People would, in turn, praise him for his benevolence.

Suddenly, Rasangam was overcome with grief. He turned away and rushed upstairs. 'Who is going upstairs this early in the morning?' amma called out, hearing his footsteps on the wooden stairs.

'It is me,' Rasangam replied, rushing into the front verandah. He sank into his father's chair and began to wail loudly. Before he had left for his last trip, Attha had seemed visibly weak. 'Attha, you need not go back. Let's just farm here. Annan and I will study well and get government jobs,' Rasangam had reassured him.

'Neither your mother nor your Mahamooda sachaani has any savings from the earnings I have sent them so far. All we have is two acres of land. How much can we farm on that, appa? My brother Basheer is no longer with us either. I am now the sole breadwinner for this family. I will go one last time and return with some money. You all should study well.'

His father's words echoed in his ears. Who knew he was never going to return?

'Open the door!' The street reverberated with Mahamooda sachaani's resonant voice. She dumped the bundle of grass that she brought in from the field in the courtyard.

'So you're back, *le*? Come, have something to eat,' Sainambu greeted her brother-in-law's wife. 'Fathima, make dosais, your mother must be hungry.'

'That can wait, I will wash up first,' Mahamooda said and went to the backyard. She drew water from the well to wash her face. Spitting out the tobacco she had tucked into her cheek, she rinsed out her mouth. Her plump body was drenched in sweat. Her robust physique and long limbs lent her a commanding presence.

'Why do you eat that disgusting thing? On top of that, you smoke *suruttu* like a man. Stinky woman!' yelled Sainambu, looking down at her from the top of the kitchen steps.

'Shut up! I do what I like, why should it bother you?' a teasing smile flickered across Mahamooda's face as she playfully argued with her co-sister.

'Your scuffles have started rather early today,' Fathima laughed, clapping her hands.

'Shut your mouth, you crazy hussy. Don't act smart!' Mahamooda shushed her daughter and sat down on the front pyol, leaning against the wall with peeling paint. She looked exhausted. 'Where is that lad, Hanifa? Has he left for the market already?'

'Here, take this, there are six dosais here,' Sainambu said, serving her. 'Are these enough or should I have her make more?'

Fathima felt a surge of panic. The anxiety of returning to the kitchen was visible on her face. Her mother noticed it and said, 'Ey, don't you make that sullen face! These are enough.' She turned to Sainambu and said, 'Come, sit here, I need to discuss something with you.'

'Eat to your fill first, we can talk later. You just drank neechuthanni at sunrise, before you left for the fields and you've only just got back – aren't you hungry?' Sainambu chided her while pouring sambhar over the dosais.

'Why are you two being so affectionate towards each other? Something is clearly terribly wrong today,' Fathima remarked.

'Just shut up for some time, won't you?' Mahamooda threw out her hand to signal her daughter to keep quiet. She retrieved neem leaves and a bunch of tulsi that she had wrapped in her sari and secured at her waist, wiped down the mortar next to the pyol and tossed the leaves into it. '*Ele*, Sainambu, bring me a bit of ginger and a lime.'

'What is all this – are you making *marundhu* now? Just relax for a minute, won't you? At least let the strain of walking all the way home wear off!' Sainambu's words were to no avail. 'Of course, as if you'll listen to me,' she murmured as she went into the kitchen and brought her some ginger and lime.

Mahamooda washed them in the water she had carried in a wide-mouthed vessel, put them into the mortar and began pounding. Ajmal, who was watching her from a distance, clutched his stomach and scrunched up his face before running to Rasangam, crying, 'Anne, marundhu!' his face dripping with the bitter memories of the herbal concoction.

Once Rasangam had accepted the inevitability of

everyone having to drink the marundhu, he shifted his attention to his aunt, who was humming a film song while pounding the herbs. Putting aside his aversion to the concoction momentarily, he was enthralled by the sight of Mahamooda singing to the rhythm of her pounding. Today, once again, the ritual would unfold: she would find them one by one, hold down their hands and legs and force the marundhu down their throats. Since there was no escape, Rasangam found it easier to just enjoy the song instead.

'Auspiciousness of the vermilion dot,
Confluence of our two hearts ...'

As she began to draw out the notes of the romantic duet, Sainambu teased her, 'Oh, it is our hero MGR's duet today. You must be in a really good mood ...'

'Of course – you remember how beautiful the couple in that song looked? We watched this movie together. It is all in the past now ...' Mahamooda let out a wistful sigh. Her voice filled the air and Rasangam watched her, enraptured.

With Mahamooda sachaani around, there was never a dull moment. In her presence, sleep was the last thing on anyone's mind. She would joke around and tease, although no one could match her ability to grasp reality and act with courage when needed.

Amma, on the other hand, was a real scaredy-cat. Everything she did was from within the sanctuary of sachaani's shadow. And that's just how impressive their sachaani was – even if the sky were to fall, she would remain unfazed. She behaved as though she controlled the whole world. Rasangam was much fonder of his sachaani than his amma.

Whenever Rasangam and Hanifa asked amma for money to go and watch a movie, she would refuse and try to dissuade them from going out at all. Sachaani, on the other hand, would not only give them money but also convince amma into letting them go. 'Was there any movie back then that we didn't go to watch? It's a phase – if they don't do this now, when will they ever?' she would tell amma, giving their plea the extra boost it needed.

When she had finally finished pounding the herbs and singing along, she sank onto the pyol with an '*Allahu*!'

'So long as you were singing away, it seems you had no thoughts of Allah,' amma teased her.

'Stop it, le,' she replied, untying and then retying her hair into a bun at the top of her head. 'I ran into that man from Ponnamaravathi at the groundnut field today. He was asking for your daughter's hand for a relative of his.'

'Which one are you talking about?' Sainambu's face contorted with confusion for a moment.

'Aabida, of course, who else?' Mahamooda said, before suddenly shooting a quick glance at her own daughter as though she had only just thought of something. Seeing no change in the expression on Fathima's face,

Mahamooda relaxed, content that she was listening to their conversation calmly.

'Aabida?! How old do you think she is? You must be mad!' Sainambu scoffed.

'Who is mad – me? This household already has two widows, one woman whose husband has abandoned her and no man to head the family. Who knows how long it will be before these boys start working in the fields and contributing to the house?'

'And what do we have to marry her off with?'

'They are keen on marrying a girl from our family. You have no reason to worry about sending your daughter away without anything, do you? And you're arguing with me over her age and all that nonsense! Tell me, at what age were you and I married off? I didn't even know how to knot the drawstrings of my petticoat properly – didn't they still send me away to live with a husband?'

Fathima sat transfixed, her mouth agape, watching the rice boil in the pot before her. Her baby Shameema slept in her lap. To the world – which was used to co-sisters perpetually at loggerheads with each other in their village – the solidarity between these two women was unbelievable. 'Have you both never once fought with each other?' Fathima had asked them one time.

'What do we have to fight over and divide between us – money? Wealth? Only chronic poverty!' Mahamooda had replied and then charged at her daughter menacingly with her hand raised as if to strike her. 'I must ward off your evil eye from us with the dirt from under your feet, *di*!'

She was now saying, 'Listen to me – they have newfound wealth. Because ours is also an important family in this village, they are asking for our daughter's hand. Sure, we are not doing too well at the moment, but they don't know that. You and I need to make this decision because if not, who else will? Ours is a household without a male head, after all.' Mahamooda sounded resolute.

Rasangam was listening closely from upstairs and was enraged by the discussion on the pyol. 'They are talking about getting a fourteen-year-old girl married?!' he mumbled to himself as he rushed down the stairs urgently, skipping every other step.

The wooden stairs shook under his footsteps as he thudded down to confront his mother, 'How can you even consider this? Why must she be married off right now? She's just in eighth class!'

'Dei, little tyke, pipe down! Can't you see us adults having a conversation?' Mahamooda shot back at him. 'That man owns a thriving grocery shop. They have enormous wealth and land to their name. You will all be set for life. Your younger brother is yet to complete his education. And then there's this one who has driven her husband away and come back here with nothing. She is one more mouth to feed. Who is going to tend to all of this?' she lowered her voice.

Rasangam yelled at the top of his lungs, 'Calm down, won't you? She is only fourteen. Surely, you are aware that the man is thirty-two. *I* will take care of her. I will study well and get a government job—'

'Dei, stop yelling. We need to weigh all the pros and cons before we decide to do something. All you ever do is talk big about studying and getting a government job!' Sainambu, who had remained quiet all this while, now finally voiced her support for Mahamooda's stance.

The morning sunlight flooding the front yard lit up the three faces and added to the heat of the moment. Outside, they could hear the sound of someone passing by, calling out, 'Anyone have any eggs available? Eggs ...'

3

ON THE DAY HE PRESENTED HIS EXCELLENT S.S.L.C. examination results to his brother-in-law, Asik, and sought his permission to pursue further studies, the weight of the keys to the grocery store falling into his hands struck his heart like a thunderbolt. When he threw them away and stomped out, his sister came chasing after him. She grabbed his hand and dragged him into a room.

'Anne, you need money to study further. How will you do it? Just accept the offer and stay here.'

He stared in wide-eyed disbelief at his sister, who had once barely known how to drape a half-sari, standing before him now in a sari and offering him advice.

'I don't need money to study further. The government will give me a scholarship so I can get an engineering degree. Periyasami sir told me – I have made all my enquiries. Back off.'

Rasangam shook free of her hands and cycled back to his village, only to return to the same place a few days later on the same bicycle to collect the keys to the grocery store.

4

Village 2

RASANGAM RESENTED HOW THE PEOPLE OF THIS VILLAGE looked down on him. Every morning, he opened the store at six, immediately after the *fajr* prayers.

The first question every customer asked him would be, 'What is your name, attha?'

'Rasangam.'

'What kind of name is Rasangam? Do Muslims really use such names?' The inquiries were elaborate, accompanied by sarcastic laughter. 'Only those who don't understand Islam or the *eemaan* would use names like Rasangam and Selvan.'

Rasangam would feel deeply humiliated. Seething with anger, he would want to snap at them that very minute to mind their own business but would calm down for fear of his brother-in-law. 'More than three quarters of this village is related to me, *maaple*. Please behave responsibly or business will suffer,' Asik's voice would sound in his ears. He reminded himself of Asik's words from the day he had first arrived. Anxiety about his inability to study further was eating away at him. He felt an overwhelming urge to lock the store, toss the keys away and simply run away somewhere.

Then the state of his family flashed in front of his eyes. He recalled Hanifa's words: 'I will manage the farmland and the coconut grove. That will be enough to run the household. You take care of yourself and ensure Ajmal's education. Our machaan is a very nice man, go help him out. He is very fond of you and knows by now that you are a responsible person.'

Rasangam studied the sacks around him: rice and lentils, and oil tins lay crammed in a disorderly fashion. The rancid odour of the oil tins suffocated him. He hadn't got used to the piercing aromas of the spices as yet, either.

Just like Mahamooda sachaani, Hanifa annan had also been practical in his approach. He was three years older than Rasangam and did not care much for his studies. His advice provided the clarity his younger cousin needed. While they had been talking, Hanifa had also been crushing some roasted split gram and sugar on the stone slab, running the stone roller over them just as deftly as Fathima would.

'What are you doing this for, anna?' Rasangam had asked.

'I felt like having a snack but there was nothing at home. So I bought some roasted split gram for a quarter of a rupee; there was sugar at home. Here, you try some too,' he had replied, offering some to his brother.

Thinking about it now made Rasangam chuckle. He thought it would be a good idea to visit his family the next day after closing the store. Two weeks had passed since he had seen everyone at home and it was infuriating not being able to go to his village – even though it was so close by – solely because he was tied up at the shop every day.

He should have been attending Pre-University College, the PUC, by now. It upset him that he was trapped working at a grocery store instead. *Allah, why have you given me a* naseeb *like this!* He lamented his fate mentally and his eyes welled up with tears. How was he to explain the reason for his tears to his brother-in-law, who was seated at the cash register?

5

RASANGAM WAS DUSTING THE CASH REGISTER THAT morning. He had to dust the entire store after he opened shop at six every day. He then had to light an incense stick by the cash register, remove the cover from the sack of salt sitting outside the shop and open it up. Because the sack would usually be left outside after hours as well, he had noticed a dog lifting its leg to urinate on it one night and had fenced the sack in using two tin planks to protect it.

At night, once machaan had counted all the money and taken it home, Rasangam would wind up the remaining work and lock up the store before going home for dinner. Aabida would serve him and make sure he ate. After dinner, he would go to sleep in a room upstairs.

Asik machaan had neither father nor mother; only a younger sister. Even though she lived under the same roof, she stayed out of his sight whenever he was home. He, in turn, did not give her much thought either.

Apparently, someone in the village had said something disdainful about their decision to take Rasangam in

– that it was a bad idea to bring a young man to live under the same roof as a girl of marriageable age. When Aabida brought this up with her brother, laughing, he looked at her closely. Her face was childlike, but there was maturity in her bearing. *How did she transform so quickly!* He could hardly believe that this was the same girl who had been perching atop the Portia tree barely a year ago. Where had her childlike spirit gone? *How much she has changed in a year! Only I have remained the same* ... Just thinking this made him choke up with sadness. But the fact that his family depended on him for putting food on the table was enough to allay his sorrows for the moment.

Every month, the family had all the groceries they needed delivered to them by the store. *If I don't take care of the shop here, I cannot send them anything. Amma will not buy anything either.* A long sigh escaped him.

Not a day went by without at least two customers taunting him. 'Rasangam, is it? Which *asarathu* gave you this name?' they would laugh. This was the one thing he had not been able to develop a tolerance for. 'Losers,' he would murmur under his breath and swallow his anger. *Attha gave me this name because of how much he loved me.*

He remembered how his father would, while cuddling him, declare over and over again that his firstborn son was going to reign over a Rasangam, a kingdom.

'Which kingdom is he going to rule over – Singapore or here?' Mahamooda sachaani would tease him.

'Either would be good enough,' Attha would reply.

'We are all but poor, humble beings. Just his name is more than enough,' sachaani would chuckle.

Attha made no distinctions between the children of the two families while buying them clothes. Both Hanifa and Rasangam grew up wearing similar outfits.

His mind was once again flooded with thoughts of Hanifa. As the desire to see him swelled yet again, he wondered how to broach the subject of going home with his brother-in-law. Just then, he heard him ask, 'How many bags of Manachanallur Ponni rice did we receive, Rasangam? Did you make a note in the accounts? Use a calculator and figure out how much we need to pay them, then make an entry in the daybook for that, pa,' jolting Rasangam back to the present.

6

WITH HIS FEET, HANIFA PLAYFULLY INTERRUPTED THE rhythm of the water flowing through the channel. . Savouring the cool breeze blowing in from the foothills as it caressed his face, his thoughts drifted to Chitra. *She comes to work in the fields every day, but I don't see her today … where could she have disappeared to?*

Whenever he thought of her, he felt a warm, uplifting sensation, as if he was soaring high up in the skies. He was filled with a longing to gaze upon her – her glistening dark skin, slender figure and large, mesmerizing eyes. She was much shorter than him. 'I only reach up to your waist,' she would groan.

He watched the crops swaying gently in the breeze under the soothing sun, enraptured. The 'sala sala' sound of the water flowing through the canal was soothing. A frog jumped out of the bund and disappeared into the crops.

Chitra's father, Sinrasu, was pulling out the weeds from the field. Feeling confident that he could inquire about her freely since Sinrasu knew nothing of their relationship, Hanifa asked him, 'How come you're here today? Why don't I see Chitra?'

Sinrasu raised his head to look at him and replied, 'That girl has a stomach ache so she couldn't come. What brings you here all by yourself today – I don't see your amma or periamma?'

'Amma and periamma said they had some work to attend to. So it's just me today.'

He was in no mood to continue the conversation and walked away. His thoughts drifted to his younger brother. *I was no good at studies – he did so well at his and yet it wasn't in his naseeb to pursue them any further. And who knows where Fathima's husband ran off to? Even when attha left us, at least periattha was there to take care of our family. Now Allah has taken him away too.* He was filled with sorrow. He sat down at the foot of a Portia tree and watched the water flowing in the channel.

He had promised Chitra that he would marry her, but he didn't know if his mother would agree to it. He was almost certain she won't.

'Get lost, you imbecile!' is all he expected to hear her say to dismiss the matter altogether.

What arrogance she has! Sainambu periamma would tease his mother, saying, 'Look at your *raangi* temper – just like a man's!'

'Will your people even allow you to marry me, an ordinary farmhand? You can't be serious …' Chitra's disbelief echoed in his ears now. But it was she who had offered him reassurance, too. 'Whatever happens, happens. Such is God's way.'

'Sendhora Poove', the song from the movie *Pathinaaru Vayathinile*, floated in on the breeze from someone's transistor radio in the distance. The movie was being screened at a nearby theatre. The other boys who had watched it had said it was really good. If Rasangam had been around, the two could have gone to watch the night show together on their bicycle.

I just don't like going alone without him. Wondering if his younger brother would visit that week, he picked up the hem of his kaili off his ankles to tie it around his waist and started on his walk home. His Bata chappals splattered mud onto his Conch-brand kaili, staining it.

'How long has this been going on?'

Hanifa grinned in response to Rasangam's question.

'First, find a way to be useful. You will get a thrashing at home if they find out! Our family already has quite the reputation in the village. And now you want romance? Rubbish! Forget about it and move on,' Rasangam grumbled as he cycled.

The increased speed of the bicycle betrayed his anger. As they rode across the small bridge, down the narrow footpath flanked by dense thorny shrubs and spiny caltrops, Hanifa stayed quiet, intently focusing on the flowing river.

'What is wrong with our family? What are you

implying?' he finally asked, sounding irritated. 'What are we lacking and who is saying what about it?'

'Oh sure, I will explain everything ... would you like a diagram to go with that too? Just shut up!'

An oppressive silence fell upon them.

'Akka's husband has run away. She is abandoned here with a child in her arms. Mother and sachaani are both widows. One of the sons has been employed at his own brother-in-law's shop to feed the family. And look at my name – Rasangam – as if I were a farm labourer! They mock our family for not knowing anything of Islam or eemaan.' Rasangam mumbled as he pedalled on, following his own rhythm. His face was red and he sounded even angrier. Hanifa, who hadn't expected his brother's disapproval, was quite shaken. He sat weighing whether or not to pay heed to his younger brother's anger.

Rasangam's appearances had transformed significantly. Hanifa noticed that his complexion too had become more radiant. *Must be from the good nutrition and sitting inside the shop, away from the sun*, he reasoned. He was amazed at how tactful and mature he had become. *It is all because of where he lives now*, he told himself. Yet, he didn't think his brother had become so wise as to offer him advice, so he remained silent.

By the time they reached the theatre, the sun had descended. 'The show starts only at 6:30, let's buy our tickets and get some tea,' Rasangam said as he started walking towards the ticket counter. When Hanifa caught a glimpse of the hundred-rupee note he was pulling out of his shirt pocket, he was taken by surprise and shrank into himself. The sight of money in the hands of his younger brother made him feel deeply uncomfortable.

'Look at your younger brother – see how smart he is? And here you are … Lazy bones!' His amma's oft-repeated words sprang to mind.

He was also reminded of the time Asik machaan had called him a wastrel. 'You think it's enough to be fair-skinned? You need to have substance, too …'

'You get the tickets, I will wait outside,' he said, slowly making his way towards the outer gate of the movie theatre premises. He noticed two young girls clad in half-saris smiling coyly, staring at him as they passed by. He returned their smiles and walked on.

He arrived at the tea stall adjacent to the gate and sat down on a bench there. Because it was close to showtime, the stall was not busy. *Sridevi is the heroine in* 16 Vayathinile, he recalled. Picking up the evening newspaper lying on the bench, he said, 'Anne, two teas, please.'

'Do you want them with cream or without?' asked the vendor.

'One regular, the other with cream,' Hanifa replied and opened the newspaper.

He and his brother enjoyed the tea made only at this particular tea stall in front of the theatre. One of the legs of the bench was broken and shook slightly. Flies buzzed around the tea spills. Hanifa got up to grab a sheet from the sheaf of newspapers hanging from the awning of the stall and wiped down the bench.

'Anna, have you ordered our tea?' Rasangam said, sitting down next to him. 'I have bought balcony tickets. It won't be crowded there.' He was wearing a new gold-plated watch around his wrist.

'Where did you get the watch, is it new?' asked Hanifa.

'Machaan gave it to me. Apparently, someone gifted it to him … It's all for a reason. I have to open the shop on time, remind him to offer prayers on time, send him home to eat on time,' Rasangam laughed.

Though darker in complexion than his cousin, Rasangam had an attractive face and physique. Hanifa patted his *thambi*'s shoulder and laughed heartily, over and over again. His explanation for the watch he was fascinated by quickly dispelled any interest he had in it. *As if that isn't a talent!* He said to Rasangam, 'That's true, too. He is always so particular about his work. Come now, drink your tea quickly and let's go, the movie is about to start.'

They hurried to leave. The earlier conversation and the anger it had provoked was all but forgotten.

Everything appeared serene in the moonlight without the streetlights. Feeling content after their movie outing, both their minds were still reeling from the visuals.

'Isn't Sridevi so beautiful?'

As a brother, and someone Rasangam was eager to confide in, Hanifa met his words with a firm nod of agreement. His mind was racing with excitement. He had come to watch a movie with his younger cousin after a long time. Back in the day, he managed to go to the talkies every week – he could even watch one every day. However, he no longer cared to go to the theatre by himself and had to wait eagerly for his brother's monthly visit.

'Why aren't you saying anything? Looks to me like you have drowned in Sridevi's beauty ...'

Hanifa teasingly rapped his younger brother on the head out of affection. 'You ride the bicycle carefully now ... Don't keep thinking about her and drown us in the pond in the dark.'

'Right now, I know that only Chitra is the epitome of beauty in your eyes, but don't let the rest pale in comparison!' Rasangam laughed and then quickly added, 'The moonlight is beautiful, isn't it?'

'Why are you changing the subject as soon as you mentioned Chitra?' Hanifa sounded disappointed.

'Falling in love doesn't mean anything. I don't want you to feel encouraged by us talking about something that is never going to happen.'

'Why do you say it'll never happen? What is wrong with it? She is ready for the *nikkah*.' Hanifa sounded agitated, which made Rasangam anxious. He knew how innocent Hanifa was – a man who believed all things white to be milk! Somebody who considered watching movies an activity par excellence in life. He considered his brother's ignorance, too, holding on to the hope of turning his fantasy into reality.

'These things don't work out in the long term. It's impossible our village will allow it to happen; just forget about her. And tell her, too, to stop nurturing feelings for you.'

Was that really his voice that had sounded so insensitive? The question and the alienness of his own voice upset Rasangam.

They were only a couple of years or so apart, but even so, they were more like twins. 'We've never seen real brothers be as inseparable as these two; they're practically joined at the hip!' the villagers teased them. Because the elder brother was naïve, he would often get duped, so Rasangam would always follow him around like his shadow. When the coconuts were plucked from their farm to be sold, Manikam Chettiar, the bulk-buyer, would try to buy the good ones at half-price, claiming falsely that they were dry. It was Picchaimani who would fight for a fair deal.

'So you tell me then: what should I do now?' Hanifa sounded faraway, like he was talking from within a well.

7

THE IMMENSE SADNESS ROSE IN HANIFA'S THROAT AND choked him. He felt abandoned by his cousin when they had always been so close. It was as if a reassuring hand had slid off his shoulder. He tried hard to supress his grief, *It won't be good if thambi comes to know about how upset I am. I'm sure he will have something more to say about that too*, he thought, holding back his tears with great difficulty.

'Do you know our family's reputation? How derisively they talk about us in the neighbouring village? They speak as though we were starving for morsels and how we live off machaan's store. They mock my name. What's more, they even say mean things about Fathima's husband abandoning her. We cannot afford to let our pride suffer any further.' He emphasized the word 'we'. His voice raw with the pain of humiliation, the indignant Rasangam pedalled on, speaking furiously.

'What is the point of ridiculing us for Fathima's husband abandoning her … such fools …' mumbled Hanifa. A dog was barking somewhere far away.

It dawned on Hanifa that he had nothing more to say.

They finally reached home. The gate to the backyard had been left unlocked for them. Letting themselves in and parking the bicycle quietly, they entered the house through the front door to find Mahamooda waiting for them in the middle of the house with food laid out before her.

'Attha, is the movie over already? How was it?' she asked with childlike enthusiasm. She griped, 'I also wanted to go, but how could I have? There are no more buses running to bring me back home. If they are screening a matinee show tomorrow, we'll go, too – what say, Sainambu?' she began serving rice onto two plates with a wooden ladle.

Earlier, the two women would go to Turing Talkies every night to watch movies. If the show was at seven, Sainambu and Mahamooda would comb their hair, put flowers in them, spray on some attar, drape Kandangi saris and leave for the theatre by five itself. Since their husbands Anwar and Basheer had both been in Singapore at the time, there had been no one to restrict them. They had to walk two kilometres to reach Turing Talkies, located in the neighbouring village.

'Look at these two sorry creatures,' the women in their neighbourhood would taunt and laugh at them. But the two of them never let that hold them back.

Sainambu alone would mutter softly, 'Ele, let's not go?'

'Adi podi … we like to go so we go. Who cares about what others say? They live with their husbands and fool around with them. Do we have ours here with us? Let's just watch movies, be happy and do as we please,' Mahamooda would say, brushing off the entire village just like that. 'Come, let's carry on. If you don't want to, just say the word. I will go by myself.' She would stand her ground.

Watching them leave their house every day with a rupee in their hand and a betel leaf pouch at their hip set the other women's tongues wagging, but it was the yearning in their eyes that Mahamooda caught out of the corner of hers as she strode past them, swinging her arms.

'Ele, they are showing the same movie they showed yesterday. Why are we going?' a reluctant Sainambu would ask, to which Mahamooda would reply, 'Would you rather we lay eggs sitting at home?'

No one in the village could afford the expense of sending complaint letters to Anwar and Basheer in Singapore to report their wives' behaviour. Once, when Basheer had been visiting, he had heard someone commenting on the two women's outings. When they had been getting intimate in bed that night, he had brought it up softly with his wife: 'Mahamooda, why do you go to Turing Talkies?'

'Don't you go to watch movies there? Yet, we shouldn't. What does it matter if we do?' Mahamooda had shot back. Basheer had had no response to that. He, too, did not really think there was anything objectionable about it since he was used to seeing women go to the movies freely in Singapore.

Every day, after they'd return from the movies, Mahamooda would sit on their pyol and narrate the story to the entire village, laughing. She would observe with pride the glint of jealousy that flashed in the eyes of the women who'd gather around to listen, hanging on to her every word, and feel pleased with herself. 'N. S. Krishnan reads out to Madhuram, standing in front of him, "There it is, right in front of me … yet how afraid I am to touch—" Just then, Madhuram's dad says, "Dei, stop, stop right there! Who are you talking about – who is right in front of you?" "Ada, why, I saw a honeycomb in the field. Even though it was on the tree right in front of me, I was afraid to touch. The honeybees would've stung me, you see … I was just sharing my sadness," he'd say and wriggle out of the situation,' Mahamooda would narrate and laugh loudly.

Once, as they were returning home after watching *Praaptham*, Sainambu remarked, 'The movie was not good at all', trying to disguise her intention of avoiding going back to see it again the next day in a barb.

'How can you say that? Do you know how difficult it is to make a movie? The cost and labour that goes into it? You think you, who are just paying thirty paise to watch it, get to call it bad?' Mahamooda was visibly angered.

'So what do you want me to do? If it's bad, it's bad ... What are you getting so worked up about?' Sainambu replied, annoyed.

However, these differences would disappear the following day and the two of them could again be seen heading to the movies together. They would make little mounds of sand on the floor of the theatre so they could squat comfortably and put the peanut candy and murukku they'd buy on their laps while they watched the movie. Once Hanifa was born, they would leave him in the care of Kattayan's wife. When Kattayan came looking for her this one time, she hastily latched the door from the outside and left the baby alone inside. By the time Sainambu and Mahamooda returned from the talkies, they found Hanifa had cried himself into unconsciousness. That was the day they stopped going to the movies. It was relegated to the occasional outing after that.

'Sure le, the boys are now at the appropriate age to enjoy the movies, why don't you go with them too? Go watch with your mouth agape,' Sainambu said, coming out of the room and settling down next to her son on the mat. She let out a loud sigh and disrupted Mahamooda's train of thought.

'What do you care how I go to the movies? It's not

like you will come with me. When I go to the market next week, I will catch the matinee show. Sheriba from the village revenue officer's house said she will accompany me.'

Hanifa and Rasangam focused on their food, turning a deaf ear to this conversation. Their minds were flooded with thoughts and ideas of their own. Unable to comprehend the silence between them, Sainambu and Mahamooda turned their attention to eating as well.

Confused and worried about what to tell Chitra kept Hanifa awake all night. He kept tossing this way and that on his mat.

'Why are you moving around so much, won't you go to sleep?' Rasangam gently nudged his elder brother's shoulder to wake him up. 'I didn't say anything wrong. I am only looking out for our family's honour. When I was in school, that girl Selvi kept hovering around me. I liked her back, but I simply let any thoughts of it wash away. Listen to me. First, sleep without guilt. Our elder sister has been abandoned and on top of that, now has a daughter as well. Your attha is no longer alive and neither is mine. You and I have to step up to protect the family.'

Hanifa listened patiently as his younger brother's whispering voice caressed his ears like a gentle breeze in the light of the moon on their terrace. *Thambi has changed so much in such a short time. He talks about family, pride and all sorts of things as if he has already acquired some social standing*, Hanifa worried. Lacking the words to handle the situation and placate his brother, he turned to lie on his back and gaze at the clouds and stars in the sky. He felt an ache in his heart. 'Okay, da, I will not think about her anymore. You can quiet down now. Stop talking so much,' he said and silenced his younger brother.

Rasangam felt a sense of relief and yet, paradoxically, no relief at all. *I must catch the first bus to the neighbouring village in the morning before pajar. I'd better get at least a little bit of sleep*, he thought as he tried to sleep and failed. The stars and clouds drifted across the sky above them. They waited for no one and had no reason to wait.

From the backyard rose the bellow of the buffalo.

8

HANIFA BEGAN TO AVOID CHITRA. RASANGAM'S COUNSEL and the family's circumstances had compounded his confusion. *No trouble would come from this wedding. Chitra is ready for nikkah. Her family, too, will not stand against us. But to worry about what the people in the village that Aabida is married into would have to say about it is a bit much*, he thought. *Why is this upstart of a young brother of mine so concerned about all that?* No matter how much he analyzed his family's reputation, he couldn't grasp the issue.

Ever since he has moved to the neighbouring village, Rasangam has completely changed the way he speaks, his image, his mannerisms – everything. No one in that village is like that – not even machaan; he is just like any other villager. Hanifa gleaned that Rasangam was doing all this in the hope of building up his prestige. *But who cares whether or not someone treats him with respect; why should he have to change himself and live a life of pretence? Why should he pass on his distress to us, too?*

It was drizzling so there was no need to water the crops. Hanifa picked up an umbrella, folded his kaili up to his knee, and set out down the street.

'Hanifa attha, where are you off to?' he heard his mother's voice call out after him.

'To the farm.'

'It's raining. There may even be thunder and lightning. Just stay home.'

'Unlikely, it's just raining. I'll be back soon,' he said, walking away.

He had taken to wearing only Rasangam's shirts and kailis these days. Rasangam had left all his old clothes with him. Their body structures were not that different. The elder brother was a little stocky and the younger one was a little lanky. Once, they went to watch a morning show of a Hindi movie dubbed into Tamil at Veera Theatre in their neighbouring village. They went to see it the day after Baashah master mentioned that there was a pair of inseparable brothers in the movie who looked just like them. It was true that there was some resemblance. He recalled now that the elder brother was played by actor Rajesh Khanna and could see why Baashah master may have thought he looked like him.

Then he thought about how Rasangam acted snobbish these days and wore tight pants just like the actor Jaishankar. 'Shrewd chap,' he murmured, secretly in awe of his thambi.

The cool breeze on the shores of the reservoir, the open fields on one side and rolling hills on the other, and the falling rain together lifted his spirits. A poem lit up his mind for a fleeting moment and he made a mental note to write it down in his notebook as soon as he went back home.

Because of the rain, not a single bee or bird could be seen in the fields. Yet, he felt overjoyed. He was fascinated by the crabs hiding away in their burrows scurrying along the edge of the banks.

If Ajmal was here, he would surely have tried to trap a few of these crabs, he chuckled.

'Why then … laughing all alone like a madman?'

Hanifa spun around at the voice behind him, startled. It was Chitra.

When he noticed how nonchalantly she was standing, getting drenched in the rain, he said, 'You're the one getting wet in the rain like a fool. Yet, you say I'm the madman.' His voice was laced with care.

'I'm a country lass. I grew up in the rain and sun. What harm can this do to me? But you are a delicate broiler chicken, better be careful,' she laughed.

'Are you making fun of me – just you wait!' He folded his umbrella, lowered it and paced over to her. 'Come, let's go sit under a tree,' he said, 'I thought you wouldn't come because it's raining.'

'I just had a feeling, that's why I'm here. If Appa sees me here, he will scold me.'

He gazed into her light eyes – they reflected the fear she felt within. Her ink-dark skin, childlike face, two braids, her skirt and half-sari – he realized that she had inexplicably become so dear to him that he couldn't possibly imagine living a life without her.

He could hear his brother's voice in his mind, saying, 'You fool! Where does she stand and where do you? Even the tallest ladder couldn't aid her in matching up to you.'

Sure, love may be blind, but must he agree with everything Rasangam says?

'A penny for your thoughts?' Chitra interrupted him.

'Nothing, really.' He placed his hands into her calloused hands and said, 'I will never abandon you.'

She couldn't fathom why he was teary-eyed, but she gripped his hands tightly and melted into tears. The rain erased their tears without a trace.

9

BROKEN BRISTLES FELL FROM THE BROOM IN Mahamooda's hand. 'You scoundrel, you know about our family, our dignity. Yet you go after the daughter of a farmhand. Tell me, why were you talking to that girl? If any of the other villagers come to know of all this, will they not spit on our faces? Foolish fellow!'

She was out of breath from her furious outburst. 'As it is your sister's husband has abandoned her and run away. She's left standing here with a girl child in her arms. No one knows where that man went. If he gets to know about this new disgrace, will he ever come back? We finally managed to marry off Aabida into a decent family. Just as we thought she was settling into a good life, you seem to have busied yourself in trying to get her thrown out of her home, haven't you?'

It was the first time Hanifa saw his mother's body shake. *When attha died in an accident, she did not shed any tears. She's that strong. Is this really her, standing in front of me trembling this way?* Forgetting to wipe the tears flowing down her face, she flung the broom into a corner, sank to the ground and slapped her forehead.

He gently placed his hand on her shoulder. 'Amma, please don't cry. I have not done anything wrong, this will never happen again,' he said and began sobbing. He sounded like a helpless child.

'My dear! My son, he is so innocent … Allah!' Sainambu rushed over to Hanifa, threw her arms around him and started crying too. Clueless about what else to do, Fathima tucked herself into a corner of the wall. Her child erupted into loud cries.

It was on the day that Chitra was married off to someone from a neighbouring village that Hanifa swallowed pesticide. As soon as the village physician's son delivered the news from the farm, Mahamooda screamed, 'My poor wretch of a son!' and ran to him, her hair wild. The village physician's son mixed salt in a cow dung solution and ran after her with it. He put Hanifa's head on his lap as he lay unconscious under a coconut tree, placed a funnel in his mouth and poured in the cow dung concoction.

Vomit spurted from his mouth as Mahamooda held his hands and wept bitterly. On the one hand, she was relieved that her son had survived, but on the other she felt anxious about what the other villagers would say when they found out. Together, both emotions flowed out from eyes as an endless barrage of tears.

10

RASANGAM CUT UP A SWEET LEMON AND SQUEEZED out the juice. He batted away the house flies swarming around him with his other hand while staying focused on the task at hand. Hanifa was seated on a hospital bed with his head hanging low, too embarrassed to face his thambi.

'Here, drink this,' Rasangam said, handing the tumbler full of juice to his elder brother.

'Leave it here, I will drink it later.' Hanifa's voice sounded feeble.

'Flies are all over it, look, they might fall into the juice. Drink it now.' It sounded like an order. A tube connected the glucose bottle to a vein in Hanifa's right hand. He extended his left hand to receive the tumbler.

Rasangam said, 'Take it in the hand you eat with and chant "Bismillah" before you drink up.'

Hanifa carefully shifted the tumbler from his left hand to his right and chanted 'Bismillah' before downing the juice. Both brothers fell silent, perplexed. Rasangam sat looking worriedly at his annan, determined not to say anything that might hurt him.

Just then, a nurse entered the room. After a moment of hesitation, she retrieved a tablet from a nearby shelf and handed it to Hanifa. 'Take this now,' she said. She stood there for a minute, looking at Rasangam, and smiled brightly. 'How much juice will you give him!' she teased before turning around to leave. He returned her smile and signalled towards the door with his eyes, requesting her to leave the room.

'Forgive me, da.' Hanifa spoke first. He was too embarrassed to look his brother in the eye. The guilt of not having paid heed to his well-meaning advice overwhelmed him.

'Forgive you for what? You are alive, that's enough for me.' Rasangam tried to free his brother from his guilt.

'I caused so much trouble for all of you.'

'Let all that be, you sleep peacefully.'

'I wanted to pursue higher studies. I wanted you to study well and get a job. But our family circumstances didn't allow it. We'll get only that which is in our naseeb,' Hanifa said.

'When I think about how abruptly my education came to an end, I also feel like I've lost my reason to go on living … so what?' Rasangam struggled to regulate his sorrow and tears, yet continued, 'Tell me, who gets the life they want? Family, circumstances, opportunities – all of this comes first. Living for yourself comes much later.'

'From now on, don't bother with such thoughts. Perform *dua* that everything in your life goes well, starting tomorrow. Think of your mother and mine. Had something happened to you, would they have been able to walk with their heads held high? Even our own relatives would have made fun of us. Right now, no one knows you poisoned yourself. We've told everyone that you were bitten by a snake. The doctor has said that he won't say anything to anyone either.'

Lying on the hospital bed, Hanifa scanned Rasangam. He was very elegantly dressed. In his trousers, held in place with a belt, and his full-sleeved shirt tucked in at the waist, he looked sharp. Even though he seemed a stranger from a distance, he exuded familial warmth when he was around. 'Okay, go to sleep now … I will also sleep for a bit,' he said, walking over to Hanifa to squeeze his hand comfortingly and went to lay down on the cot across from him.

'How is annan?' Aabida asked in a whisper. She sounded tired. Asik was eating his dinner in the kitchen.

'He is fine,' Rasangam whispered and walked towards his room.

He heard the jingle of bangles from behind a curtain. He understood that it was Banu hiding because of him. 'I don't want anything to eat. Let machaan know that I have come back,' he said before entering his room and locking it. Now Banu was free to walk around the hall.

Aabida had figured out that Banu made her bangles jingle to attract Rasangam's attention. She would say to him, 'Banu talks only about you all the time. When I came here after my marriage, do you know how arrogantly she used to behave just because she's my sister-in-law? But these days, she's all grins around me. It's all because of you.'

'Shhh! Pipe down, won't you?' Rasangam would reply.

'I'm telling you the truth. Ever since machaan mentioned that he's thinking of getting you both married, she's been like this. Allah has protected me,' Aabida would wink.

'Why, what is the rush to get me married?' he would say wearily.

'He really wants to marry her off to someone outside the village. But do you know what the whole village says? That who will marry a girl with no mother? Who will then cater to the expectations of her in-laws? That's why.'

He found the way the people of this village talked perplexing. 'So even if a girl is wealthy, they wouldn't marry her if she doesn't have a mother? Such fools!' he would say with disgust.

'One needs the girl to have a mother to take care of her when she is pregnant, bring up her child, arrange for gifts for all life events, spoil the son-in-law. Otherwise, it all ends with the wedding. You think the girl's sister-in-law, her brother's wife, would allow him to bear all the additional expenses on her account for the rest of her life? The girl needs her mother to indulge the son-in-law's whims afterwards.'

'Ey, you shut up. Don't talk like an old woman. That too the women of this village. You've started sounding more and more like them; it's sickening,' he would say to shut her up.

'If you come to live in a village that eats fish, you take your share and move on,' she would mock him. Time and circumstance could change anyone into anything, or so it seemed. Even though there was a wide age gap between machaan and Aabida, neither had expressed any discontent on that account.

Amma would say, 'Bear one child and you will become all kinds of smart. But what is one to do – such a time has still not emerged on the horizon for the two of them.'

'She herself is a child. Why should she rush into bearing one?' Hanifa would spring to his cousin's defence.

'Dei, you stay away, what does a man know about all this that you've come to speak for her? As though your sister doesn't know how to bite a finger that's slid into her mouth,' Mahamooda would chide her son.

Rasangam undressed, hung his clothes from a hanger and lay down on the bed. Thoughts of Hanifa filled him. Oh, the cruelty of trying to end one's life over the misplaced belief that something impossible was, in fact, true love!

We owe it to someone else's good deeds that he has survived … Che! Why am I using terms like 'good deeds' like the villagers say, like I am a kafir. He bit his tongue wondering how long it would take him to change his ways. *Hanifa gets to live another day because of someone's dua*, he corrected his thought.

After Asik machaan finished his dinner and retired to bed, Aabida soundlessly entered her brother's room, hugged him and began to weep for Hanifa. The night brought with it the worry and anxiety of keeping their sorrow under wraps.

11

'WHERE ARE YOU GOING TO SEND AJMAL?'

When amma raised the question, Ajmal stood trembling in his scrawny body. A glimmer of hope flickered in his face that his amma might intervene and save him.

'To a school with hostel facilities,' Rasangam declared his decision firmly.

'Allah! What is that?'

'Hmm, he can stay there and study.'

'And then ...?' Sainambu asked in despair.

'He will visit us once every three months. And then he can come home for vacation after his final exams.'

Sainambu started crying loudly. 'Why do you have to send him now? He's still a child, will he not miss us?'

'You think he is still a child? Will you stop creating a fuss?' Rasangam chided her sternly, projecting an authoritative front.

Mahamooda was lying on the pyol outside with her arm folded under her head. Her eyes were fixed on the beam above. It was clear she was deep in thought.

Feeling betrayed that she had not sprung to her

defence as yet, Sainambu yelled out to her from the inner courtyard. 'Ele, Mahamooda, come and see what is going on here! This boy is saying something I can't make sense of at all! Are you daydreaming over there?!' she reproached her.

Rasangam was alarmed at his mother's volume. He was so used to seeing her as soft-spoken, watching her get this angry had left him tongue-tied. He had already guessed all this might happen. He was also prepared for Mahamooda to take his mother's side. He had a response ready for what she might say as well.

'Why, what is going on here?' Mahamooda sat up, rearranging her crumpled sari properly across her chest. 'I have a headache. That's why I thought I would lie down for some time. Rasangam attha, what are you saying? Are you really going to send him away?' she sounded frustrated. The brilliance and enthusiasm she used to radiate had disappeared.

The fear of Hanifa harming himself again had taken root in her. She kept him close to her and protected him fiercely like a brooding hen does her eggs. This gave Hanifa comfort too. Rasangam also had instructed his sachaani not to leave him by himself. It was Picchaimani who had informed him that Chitra had been married off and sent to live with her husband in his village.

'I am talking to you, dear, why are you standing still as a tree?' Mahamooda's voice brought him back to the present.

'Yes, he will get a good education. We didn't get the opportunity,' Rasangam replied with conviction.

Ajmal sat down quietly. He did not want to leave his village and live far away from his mother, but he could not challenge Rasangam. He was the one who decided everything. When amma and sachaani themselves had not been able to convince him to change his mind, he didn't know what he could do about it. He only knew to cry, but he wasn't sure if that would move his brother either.

'Where is Hanifa?' Rasangam realized just then that Hanifa had been missing the whole time.

'He is sitting on the terrace; he doesn't talk to anyone,' Mahamooda answered bitterly.

'I will talk to him.'

'We have found a bride for him,' said Mahamooda. Her tone indicated that he was not to interfere in the matter. *You are a mere sapling and you have no right to poke your nose into these matters*, it seemed to say. He climbed up the stairs without a word.

Hanifa was lying on his back in the evening sun. Rasangam went up to him and asked softly, 'Why are you lying here in the sun, anne?'

Hanifa, awakened by the sound of his cousin's voice, took his time sitting up. Rasangam was relieved to find that the hot floor slab underneath him was endurable. Hanifa's reddened face glistened with sweat. 'If you sweat like this, won't you catch a cold? Why are you lying around like this?'

'I won't catch anything. I have neither work nor responsibility, that's why I'm lying here. Since amma has given away the coconut grove on lease, I have no work to take care of, that's all,' he answered wearily.

'I keep telling you to come join machaan's store, but you don't listen to me. We are planning to set up a cycle spare parts store as well; you could take care of that.'

'How would that be possible? Doesn't this house need a man? Also, I won't come to live in that village. They're an arrogant lot.' His dislike surfaced as he spoke.

'Okay, okay ... come, let's go inside.' Rasangam extended his hand to help him up.

His body was soaked in sweat. The purple shirt he was wearing stuck to his back. It was upsetting to see him like that.

Although he could not be bothered, he did not want to dismiss his brother, so Hanifa stood up, retrieved his hand from his brother's clasp and wore his kaili properly. There was nothing but bitterness in his heart.

Hearing footsteps coming up the stairs, the two men turned their heads to see who it was from where they were sitting in the small upper room. Fathima emerged, wearing an old voile sari. The glass bangles on her wrists, the black bead strung in a gold chain around her neck and her hair tied into a bun made her look stunningly beautiful. 'Come, akka,' Rasangam greeted her. Her dark green eyes darted around uncertainly on her round face. Going by her body language, it seemed she had come to share her younger brothers' suffering.

The three of them sat down on a mat spread on the floor. Because the room they were in was adjacent to the open terrace, it had trapped the heat radiating from it and become insufferable. Fathima got up and turned on the fan. Thick, hot air enveloped the three of them.

'What was your mother talking about? Why marriage; who is the girl; what is the rush?' Rasangam directed a volley of questions at his cousin.

'Yes, these two women went over to meet our Bhaikaaramma's daughter, discussed the details and fixed everything.'

'What did you say?' Rasangam asked Hanifa.

'"Why must I get married?" But no one listens to what I say,' his voice trembled, his eyes teary.

'Of course, it's because he's always lying around staring at the roof. Amma is afraid he will do something stupid again like he did the other day—'

Rasangam cut her off, 'Shhh … don't say that, akka.'

Hanifa sat still and unmoved. Rasangam remembered amma mentioning that ever since Hanifa had returned from the hospital, he'd been making loud noises at night. Had he been possessed by the devil? Amma had called him once and asked him if she should take Hanifa to the mosque in Ervadi or Kadva. Rasangam had got mad at her. 'Don't you all get together and make a madman out of him!'

After that, no one told him anything. But they had tied a couple of small talismans around his waist. Rasangam had noticed them when Hanifa was fixing his kaili.

'The girl is beautiful. She lost her father and they can barely afford a meal every day. They told her they didn't expect any dowry. Besides, who wouldn't like to marry Hanifa?' Fathima laughed, hugging Hanifa's shoulders.

Even then, Hanifa showed no movement. 'Where is Ajmal going?' he asked.

'I am going to enrol him in a school. They have a hostel, too.'

'That would be expensive, who is going to bear the costs?' Hanifa sounded concerned.

'Machaan offered to pay for everything. Let him study well and get a good job. The two of us couldn't afford to.' Rasangam's voice sank in frustration.

'Just because he offers, should we just accept? Won't our sister's relatives hold this favour over her head in the future?' Fathima asked in irritation, exposing her secret wish that Ajmal wouldn't leave. She was determined to try and stop Rasangam from sending the child away because it would bring her unbearable sadness to be separated from him. *Ajmal is the only playmate my daughter Shameema has.*

'Why do you say that, akka? Here I am thinking of Ajmal's well-being. Like amma and sachaani, you too are more worried about what Aabida's in-laws will say. Who else is in machaan's family? He has neither a father nor a mother, nor any elder siblings.'

'The whole village will gossip about us.'

'How will they find out about all this? He is going to study at a school close to Madurai. Who are we going to discuss the details with?'

Hanifa and Fathima observed his intensity and how his words erupted from the pit of his stomach. It frightened them.

'Okay, okay, don't get so worked up. Come, let's all go and eat,' Fathima placated her cousin.

'What are you going to do?' Rasangam asked Hanifa.

'Amma is really worried about him ever since that day. You stay out of it, Rasangam. If he gets married and settles down happily, that will bring relief both to amma and periamma.' Fathima responded despite not being asked, just to try and put a stop to the conversation. That was the reason she had wanted them to get moving as well.

Hanifa, taking cue from his sister's distress, stood up and said to his younger brother, 'Come. Let's go eat.'

Plagued by his unanswered questions and confusion, Rasangam climbed down the steps with his cousins.

12

RASIYA WAS LIKE A DELICATE BLOSSOM. AABIDA COULDN'T stop looking at her. *They say her family struggles to put food on the table. Yet, it is in such a family that this beauty has bloomed!* she mused.

'What are you doing there, sitting next to the bride? Come here and serve food to your husband,' Sainambu called out to Aabida from the kitchen while adjusting her headscarf to fully cover her head.

'Coming, amma,' Aabida said, getting up.

Hanifa was lying on a mat in the living room. She went up to him and said, 'Anne, go to your room and talk to anni. She is all by herself,' pinching his cheek affectionately before leaving.

Hanifa neither responded to her, nor did he get up. Rasangam had gone to the neighbouring village to buy things for the post-wedding *valima* feast they were hosting. Being married felt like bearing a very heavy burden to Hanifa. Neither happiness nor hatred could describe his state of being. He could not understand why a darkness was expanding in his mind. It became a struggle to push away that greasy darkness.

I feel sorry for that girl. He recalled how she had sat trembling with fear next to him the night before. He had fallen asleep feeling sorry for her.

The aroma of meat and delicacies for the feast wafted through the air, caressing him. Aabida stopped briefly on her way to the staircase, carrying food for machaan.

'Anne, you and anni get ready to eat. Once machaan finishes eating, I will serve you two.' She was wearing a sari with sparkling zari. Her voice was laden with mirth. 'Go and chat with her,' she urged him again and started climbing up the stairs, laughing.

'Ey … you be careful now, the steps are narrow. Don't trip over your sari,' Hanifa warned his little cousin.

'Okay, anne!'

'Sit up, attha, don't you have to eat?' Mahamooda's voice prompted Hanifa to sit up. Her face was glistening with sweat and radiant from contentment. She wiped her face dry and said, 'Go, attha, and talk to the girl. She is sitting alone by herself in there, isn't she?'

Acknowledging his amma's unease, Hanifa got up and walked into his room. Rasiya, seated at one end of the iron cot, stood up hastily when she saw him. 'Sit down,' he said as he settled down on the cot himself.

'Their match is simply superb – like the movie stars Shivaji and Padmini!' someone had remarked to Mahamooda the day before.

To that, she had laughed and replied, 'Indeed! I have found someone perfect for him, even though her family didn't have money or means.'

There was only one thing on his amma's mind: to stop Hanifa from fretting over his lost love. That was her only reason to arrange this marriage. He recognized she had thought it all through as best as she could – even though her family was poor, she ensured the girl she found for him was beautiful. Whatever his mother's wishes were, he desired to fulfil them.

Rasiya sat with her head lowered. Her face was concealed by her headscarf.

'No one else is here except me. You can look up or your neck might start hurting.'

'Hmm,' she responded with a feeble monosyllable. She liked that he cared about her. Feeling content about spending her life with him, she looked up straight at him and smiled. Her large nose pin with sparkling gemstones, like Sridevi's, made her look particularly lovely. He was reminded of the actress and the movie *16 Vayathinile.*

13

'COME AND EAT!' BANU SHOUTED, STANDING AT THE bottom of the stairs. Her voice was loud enough to be heard seven houses from theirs.

'Coming! And please speak softly, it hurts my ears,' Rasangam said, climbing down the stairs.

'The dosais are getting cold and you rush only if I yell,' Banu laughed, walking towards the dining table. The shouting had left her panting.

'I'm almost there,' Rasangam replied, walking down the wooden steps slowly. The smell of the attar that he had smeared on himself filled the dining room.

'Allahve! Why have you used so much attar? This smell is going to give me a headache. How many times do I have to tell you not to do that?' Banu said, serving him a dosai, and sat down on the dining chair across from him.

Although she looked tired, she was dressed in a zari-adorned sari and a lot of jewellery. 'What is the occasion for the lady to be dressed so fine?' Rasangam asked tactfully and then chanted 'Bismillah' before he began eating.

'I have to go to the street adjacent to ours. Sayiba's

daughter's engagement and poochoodal ceremony is happening there today. I feel faint just looking at how the sun is beating down outside,' she said, sounding bored.

Rasangam's face betrayed his disdain.

'What was with that look?' she asked in playful anger.

'Nothing, really. It's just that for a person who sounds so tired of it all, you are quite decked up. Couldn't you opt for something simpler?'

'Oh, this is to enhance your reputation. The village needs to know how you pamper your wife, covering her in jewellery from head to toe. That's right … as though that's not important to you!'

He quickly finished eating while listening to his wife affectionately.

'Should I make you more dosai?' she asked.

'You have maintained your full figure eating on my behalf as well, why would I want more?' he teased her. He washed his hands chanting 'Alhamdulillah'. 'Shall I ask the driver to drop you? No, wait, just walk there, that will be better. You will get some exercise. Cover yourself fully with the dupatti. Don't wear it for the sake of …' He was amazed at how uncharacteristically softspoken he was with her. If he raised his voice or ordered her around, she would unleash a tempest on him. By the time their drawn-out fights would resolve, going to the shop to get any work done would be futile.

'Don't you worry, we cover ourselves properly here,

that is how principled my family is. You make sure your skullcap doesn't get blown away by the wind. If this isn't like the nouveau riche teaching the way of the world to people with generational wealth.'

Her sharp words struck their target in his heart. No one could match her ability to annihilate him or his lineage in a second. He felt hurt.

Honour – how much this word has hounded me all my life, he tried to recall.

Would he ever be able to forget how the village had mocked him when Asik machaan had entrusted him to look after the entire store just as he had arrived to work for him?

'Look at how luck has favoured this uncouth nobody from some godforsaken village! What a matter of honour and prestige it is to man the cash register of Illahi store. And the lad's managed to grab hold of that seat just like that! The life Asik's father, the elder Kajamogaideen, had led, the respect he had earned, the way he had sat elegantly at the cash counter and the stateliness of his manners … Does it look good giving all that hard-earned prestige away to a random brother-in-law?'

They had gossiped within earshot of Asik and Rasangam. Asik seemed to not even notice them. He also had harboured the intention of getting his orphaned sister married to Rasangam. It was all part of his plan: to give him the grocery store first and his sister later.

Aabida had told her brother once before, 'Machaan

wants to get Banu married to you. She is a bit strong-headed. A motherless child, she's been spoiled to bits. Other than that, she would be a good match for you.'

Even though Rasangam had not found it agreeable, he had remained silent on the matter. The mere thought of the villagers here had infuriated him. *They look at us condescendingly and call us uncouth as if they live in London themselves. Idiots! All that arrogance just because they have money. Not a single college in the area, not even a decent hospital, yet somehow this is better than a hamlet?* He would say to himself, his blood boiling, but he would never discuss it with anyone else. *Doing my work diligently is the only way I can do justice to the trust machaan has placed in me. What else can I do?*

'What are you busy thinking so deeply about that you don't even notice someone is standing in front of you?' Farooq's voice snapped him out of his thoughts.

'Sorry, I didn't see you there,' he said, opening the store for the day. Even though he usually opened the store at eight sharp, he was late by a quarter of an hour today. *So what, this isn't exactly an office job*, a thought darted across his mind.

His thoughts drifted back to machaan's oft-repeated words. 'I cannot sit here in the store all day. My buttocks will not allow it. Half the time, it was the accountant who was taking care of everything here, I knew whatever he kept track of to be the accounts. It is only after Rasangam started overseeing the store so responsibly that I am seeing so much profit.' Words that carried no remorse for having destroying his dreams of becoming an IAS officer. He, on the other hand, had been drowned in pain and sadness and would secretly wipe away the tears that escaped his resolve.

Why am I thinking about all that now? He stopped himself from getting more upset over bygones and chanted 'Bismillah' as he opened the cash register.

The movie *Vaazhve Maayam* had just been released. The songs were good so he had bought the cassette tape when he had gone to Madurai the day before to bulk-buy goods for the store.

'No one else has a tape recorder here. You are the first one to have bought it. How is it that it repeats exactly what we say?' Banu had asked in astonishment. His explanation had fascinated her. *I should take the cassette and tape recorder when I go home tonight. I can listen to the songs at night.*

The telephone rang, bringing him back to earth. '*Salaam alaykum* … Attha, are you well?' It was Mahamooda sachaani, she sounded distressed.

'*Wassalaam.* What is it, sachaani?'

'Attha … I can't find Hanifa. Don't know where he's gone. He and I were both sleeping at the Ervadi mosque. I woke up this morning and he was gone. What am I to do!' The sobbing voice on the other end of the line crushed him.

'Don't cry, sachaani. I will come there immediately.'

He suddenly realized that although he was reassuring her, he had also started crying along with her. *Why did they go to Ervadi?* he wondered, befuddled and concerned, but he controlled his urge to question her. 'You go back home. I will find him one way or another,' he reassured her and put the phone down. Tears rolled down his face.

14

'I AM LEAVING, PLEASE TAKE CARE OF THE STORE. Hanifa has gone missing again.' Rasangam informed machaan as he prepared to leave.

'What happened – Hanifa is missing?' Asik asked, his face overcast with sadness.

'Yes, I will go by car and come back as soon as I can,' Rasangam said as he left the store.

The car was parked in the neighbourhood. It was within walking distance from the store, so he walked hastily; his body was shaking with fear. Hanifa went missing this way at least once every six months.

Reaching the car, he got in and checked to see if there was enough fuel. Satisfied, he turned on the ignition. He did not want to tell Banu about this. *She would blurt it all out to Aabida. Why make her anxious too? Let me first find him, then I'll come back home and tell her everything.* He knew he could trust Asik machaan to not say anything.

He drove his Ambassador car to the village adjoining his, like he usually did. The one where he and Hanifa used to go to watch movies. The road from his village forked into two, one that led to this one; the other led to machaan's. He doubted that Hanifa would have come to machaan's village to see him, so he decided to drive to the village with the movie theatre first.

Rasangam was the first one in machaan's village to own a car and to learn how to drive it and was rightfully extremely proud of it. He wished to show the village that disrespected him what he was made of and that he was the better man.

'So, the big shot has bought a car and drives around in it – he's like that man with meagre means from a story, who comes into a bit of luck and buys an umbrella, proudly holding it open over his head even in the dead of night,' Sayyed and Bakrudeen had remarked at the mosque, knowing he could hear them. *That is how they deal with their jealousy*, he had disregarded them and practised *sabr* to help restrain himself. *No matter what you do, we will not respect you* is what the village's gossip seemed to tell him. He had tried not to be too bothered by it.

It had been eight years since he had moved there. It was unbearable how they still treated him like an outsider even though he was now married to someone from the village and was raising his own family there.

He did not discuss Hanifa with Banu.

'Why do you care so much about your brother?' she would say. 'Your brother this, your brother that – it's all you ever talk about,' he recalled the annoyance in her voice when she said that.

What does she know about our closeness? He shrugged off her voice, parked the car on a street close to the movie theatre and walked to it via a narrow lane. It reeked of urine and cow dung. The place had not changed much in the last eight years. They had, however, painted the theatre. The movie *Vaazhve Maayam* was being screened.

He reminisced about how he and his brother had watched *Moondram Pirai* and cycled the whole way home discussing Sridevi's beauty. He found himself at the tea stall adjacent to the theatre – the same one where they usually had tea together. He looked around for the tea master, but there was just a little boy in there.

The clay tile roof above the shop had now been replaced with a moulded concrete one. The area in front was paved with mosaic flooring and there were plastic chairs on it. They had clearly put in a lot of effort into giving it a more modern appearance.

'What appa, Rasangam, are you well? It's been a while. What brings you here?' Ganesan emerged from the shop. 'Would you like some tea?' he asked. He could see there was hot water in the boiler.

His voice returned Rasangam to the present. 'Anne, are you well?' he enquired. He noticed that Ganesan was wearing a string of prayer beads around his neck, indicating he was keeping a vow.

Why was he feeling so burdened by thoughts from his past?

'Did my brother come by here?' Rasangam tried to sound casual, concealing his agitation.

'Yes, I saw him around eight this morning. His clothes were dirty. He was wearing his kaili folded. He should be here somewhere near the theatre, where else would he go?' Ganesan's voice was loaded with pity.

Realizing he was rather familiar with the matter that he was trying so hard to hide, Rasangam thanked him and entered the theatre through the iron gate beside the stall.

The sun was blazing fiercely overhead. He approached the ticket counter and looked around the area. Hanifa was standing at the counter. He looked proud, standing first in line. In that stuffy, poorly ventilated space, his face was drenched in sweat.

'Anne,' Rasangam said, stepping into the queue area.

Hanifa spun around, hearing his voice and said, 'Rasangam! Come, come, let's watch a movie. There's a good movie showing now.' His face brightened at the sight of his brother and he beckoned him with open arms.

Rasangam's eyes welled up. Hanifa looked so dishevelled that he could barely recognize him. His hair was matted and his clothes tattered. 'Anne, why are you here? Come, we will come back in the evening to watch the movie. Let's go home now, amma is looking all over for you,' he said.

'Is that so … no movie now? Okay, if you say so,' he said obediently, as though bound by his thambi's words. Smoothing down his hair, he walked briskly towards

Rasangam. He caught hold of his hand, ready to start walking with him. Rasangam led him outside. He tightly clutched Hanifa's bone-dry palms and walked towards his car. On their way, Rasangam stopped at the tea stall and ordered two teas and buns for his brother. He filled an aluminium tumbler with water from a mud pot there, took his brother to a corner and washed his face and hands; his teeth were stained.

'Why did you go to the *dargah* with amma?' he asked him softly.

'As if … it was that Saroja Devi who dragged me there.'

That was what Hanifa called Mahamooda to tease her when he was in a good mood. Rasangam turned away to wipe the tears rolling down his face. His brother sounded tired.

'I am hungry, Rasangam … hurry up and get me a bun,' he said.

'Wait. You can eat only after you've washed your hands. Rub them together well. I will pour some water,' he said, unwrapping a piece of two-rupee soap hanging from a string at the shop and giving it to him. 'Here, take this and wash up properly.'

Ganesan served the tea he had made for them and fixed his worried gaze on the two brothers. He felt very distraught. He had known them since they had been kids. Seeing them suffer like this was unbearable for him.

Luckily, there was not much of a crowd at the shop. *People must have gone to the weekly market in the neighbouring village*, Rasangam assumed.

Hanifa stuffed a whole bun into his mouth. No one could tell when he had last eaten anything. Rasangam opened a credit account at the shop with the standing instruction that Hanifa be given whatever he asked for whenever. Once, because he had approached the corner shop for some tea, the shop boy Yusuf had got annoyed and poured hot water on Hanifa. After that incident, Rasangam had decided he would set up an account at Ganesan's shop.

Why is my mind in such a turmoil? What is this life; why are we plagued by all these troubles? Whose sins are we paying the price for? He agonized. *Why did that girl Chitra set herself on fire? If her husband tortured her and beat her up, was that reason enough to die? Why should that death have affected him so deeply? Was it not I who had stopped Hanifa from getting married to her? Maybe that is why I'm so riddled with guilt.*

But could I have really let that wedding happen? How was it even an option? Would amma or sachaani have agreed to it? Would the village have accepted it? Rasangam tried his best to rid himself of his guilt, but it was in vain.

Hanifa was sipping the piping hot tea without a pause. 'Drink slowly, it's hot,' he said.

'No, the temperature is just right,' he replied and went on drinking. Rasangam shuddered with despair as he sat watching his brother drink the tea.

Tears blurred Ganesan's vision as he stood watching them, overwhelmed.

It was dark by the time they reached home. Rasangam had waited to avoid entering the village before nightfall. Hanifa said to his brother with unusual coherence, 'Not sure why, but sometimes something happens to me. I scream at night. Amma thinks I am possessed. She then forces me to go with her to these places and torments me.'

15

WHILE MAHAMOODA SOBBED HUGGING HER SON, RASIYA stood holding a pillar, her head lowered. Rasangam noticed how she showed no sign of distress. Her face had become pale. Her eyes watched Hanifa with great indifference. They were not prepared to shed any tears.

It was Rasangam's amma who made the preparations for Hanifa to take a bath, ranting under her breath the whole time. Fathima was in the yard, adding charcoal under a pot to heat the water for his bath. Standing next to her was Shameema, clutching her mother's sari.

Her mother's tears made Fathima cry too.

'Calm down, sachaani. Let's first get him to take a bath, give him some food, let the rest of the family also spend time with him. Stop crying now,' Rasangam said.

Mahamooda quietened down, sensing the sternness in his voice. She pressed the loose end of her sari firmly against her face to dry her tears. She then asked Hanifa, 'Where did you go, attha, do you know how long your amma searched for you? Why did you leave without telling me, attha?'

'Did you think I got lost? I was only stretching my feet along market street. When thambi called to me, I came home. Please don't cry,' he explained patiently, as though nothing had happened.

At least this time, we found him the very next day after he disappeared and brought him home right away. The last time this had happened, it had taken us four days to find him! It is all Allah's grace. Rasangam thanked Allah in his mind. He was more troubled by Rasiya. He could not fathom what she wanted and that was eating away at him. It felt cruel watching her stand there detached, as though she was a stranger. Her gaze was fixed firmly on the wall. There was not a trace of tears or sympathy in her deep blue eyes.

Rasangam lowered his head. Both amma and sachaani were too busy grumbling to notice anyone else. 'Hanifa anne, look, machi has been watching you,' he said. He was intent on disrupting her apparent peace. She turned her head towards Rasangam and smiled quietly, understanding his intent. Behind her smile lay an ocean of sorrow; it crushed him.

'Rasiya! Come, sit here. Your feet must hurt, you've been standing there for a while,' Hanifa, seemingly returning to his senses, waved his arm and invited her over.

Hesitating for a second, not knowing what to do, Rasiya ran into her room the next instant, locked the door and broke down crying. The sound of her whimpers deluged Rasangam's ears.

Rasiya could not sleep. Her mother-in-law and Hanifa had gone to Ervadi, even as Fathima had tried to stop them. 'Hasn't Rasangam forbidden you from going to such places? Why are you taking him to the dargah and torturing him like this?' She recalled how distraught Fathima had seemed, looking at her brother.

She came out of her sweltering room.

Fathima was asleep in her room with Shameema. The bright moonlight that bathed the courtyard, together with the cool breeze against her skin, stirred a quiet arousal in her. She shivered slightly. The hunger and the longing she felt brought Rasangam to mind, not Hanifa. When she thought about the way he spoke, his physique and his gaze, she felt as if she might lose her mind.

She had started falling in love with him without even realizing it. Now she didn't know what to do with her fixation with him. She wished to keep it hidden from others, but it took an enormous amount of effort to keep it to herself. Despite her constant, deep-seated fear that Fathima might discern where her heart lay from her actions, she took care to keep her love concealed. Waiting eagerly for the days when he would visit and trying to communicate her feelings for him with just her gaze, while ensuring no one else noticed, was not easy. He did not have the courage to look at her directly, always struggling, faltering and avoiding her gaze – she enjoyed that.

On the days she struggled to fall asleep, only thoughts of Rasangam kept her company. She did not wish to control her heart's longing for him. She only welcomed the relationship she had with him in her thoughts with great pleasure and never once did she consider her daydreams to be sinful or fear that in her afterlife, they might render her answerable to God and lead her to the gates of Hell. She desired to live only in the moment.

16

'WHERE DO YOU RUN OFF TO EVERY NOW AND AGAIN?' Fathima asked Hanifa as she dried his hair with a towel. Her voice trembled as she spoke.

'No ma … I leave thinking I'll go for a walk. I just forget the way back home. See, Rasiya has stopped talking to me now. Please tell her that I don't go away willingly. It's the devil who whisks me away somewhere.'

Fathima was amazed. *He speaks with such clarity, has he really become unstable? He does all his work by himself, he talks coherently. Then what is it that makes him lose control time and again and how does he get lost? It's inexplicable – amma has checked to see if he is influenced by black magic so many times already. On some nights, he screams 'Aiyo, fire – it's hot, it's hot!' and runs off to crouch in a corner of the room. He's already wearing multiple talismans. When Hasanamma from South Street suggested it, amma even took him to the Ervadi dargah on Friday night and spent a few days there. It is only since they have returned from there that he's got worse. He's been talking to himself more and disappearing more often. Rasangam had begged her not to take him there. 'The dargah is dirty, go to the hospital instead,' he'd said. But amma did not listen to him.* Her mind was wilting from the pain. *What else is this life going to bring and upon whom?*

Rasiya had said to her, 'I don't have another place to go. I will simply continue living here for the sake of food – this is the life meant for me, just as you live.' When she had said it, her voice had been clear. Perhaps it would be more accurate to say that Fathima sensed, rather than understood, that there was a resolve in Rasiya to let despondency take root.

The two women had developed a deep bond built on closeness and mutual understanding. Rasiya was a woman just like her. Both their lives were plagued with failure. What else did they need when they had each other?

When Fathima bent down to wipe Hanifa's legs, she saw dark, swollen bruises around his ankle as if from being chained. Rattled, she gently touched them.

'Aah! That hurts!' he shouted.

'What happened? How did this happen?' she panicked.

'You know that mosque somewhere that amma took me to and had me chained – that's how I got hurt. I'm not mental, ma! This is why I ran away,' the helplessness in his voice brought Fathima to tears.

'It's those women who are mental! I kept telling them over and over again not to take you to Ervadi, but did they listen to me? Now they've completely destabilized this child,' she murmured. 'Wait, I will bring some ointment to apply on your wounds,' she said to him and went to the kitchen. When she returned, Hanifa was deliberately scratching his wounds. Blood was oozing from them.

17

BANU'S HIGH-DECIBEL VOICE WAS AN INDICATION THAT Imran was getting ready for school. Even though he wanted to ask if all the drama was necessary, Rasangam chose to keep quiet. *She will pounce on me. Why court trouble?* He ate silently. He had put on a cassette in the tape recorder, but he could not enjoy the music amidst all the noise. The rushing around and fuss while getting Imran ready for school was an everyday ritual. He felt bad for his son. The chaos … and he was only in second class!

'Attha, *you* help me get ready for school from now on. This amma shouts too, too much!'

He chuckled now as he recalled what Imran had whispered into his ears without his mother's knowledge and choked on his food.

'What are you thinking about while eating?' Aabida rushed over to him to pat his head and handed him some water from a *sombu*.

'Nothing,' he said to placate her as he drank the water.

'Why do you need music while you eat? It's just music, music, music all the time,' Aabida grumbled aloud as she made her way to the kitchen. She had gained quite a bit of weight and walked with effort. Rasangam worried that her excess weight might lead to knee issues.

'Allahu!' Banu exclaimed as she sat down on the pyol outside their house. 'By the time I send him off to school, I am completely wiped out. The little devil!' Her face and body were drenched in sweat.

'It is simply beyond me how someone can feel exhausted by this,' Aabida's voice sounded like a rebuke. 'Here we are, yearning to have children and you sit there complaining about having one.'

Not knowing how to respond, Banu kept quiet.

Aabida's face showed concern. She wondered if she had said something wrong. Rasangam, who was sitting at the dining table and watching the scene unfold, panicked. 'Uh, Banu, I want my tea. Can you please quickly bring me some? I have to leave.'

'I'll be right there,' Banu responded, realizing that he had given her an escape from the awkward situation. She got up and rushed towards the kitchen.

Aabida, too, understood why her brother had sent Banu off on a chore. It was his way of defusing the tension between the two women whenever they got into the occasional spat. Banu would accuse Aabida of being jealous of her because she had a child. Such things happened often. She couldn't always come up with a retort to Banu's impudence, so she would just stay silent. She never knew what might set her off around Banu.

She went into her room. 'If she scolds her child, why must I interfere and try to defend him? I can't seem to learn how to hold my tongue, the devil ...' she chided herself, making great effort to keep her troubled mind and tears to herself.

It's been a while since I've been back home. It would be nice to go and spend some time with everyone, she thought. But she knew that when she went there, the people in the village will kill her with questions about why she hadn't had any children yet. 'Oh Allah!' she sighed making her way to the well to perform *olu* and cleanse herself in preparation for prayers.

Rasangam, still seated at the dining table, was very stressed. *Why is she performing olu now*, he wondered, watching Aabida.

Should praying be limited to specific times? She can pray and chant whenever she feels like it. That is good too, isn't it?

He decided it was best to let her find peace in whichever way she could. He took out his TVS 50 to go to the shop. Thoughts of Hanifa were piling up in his mind. He made a mental note to call his amma when he reached the shop. But why was he struggling to get Rasiya's face and eyes out of his mind? The thought of what her future might look like grew into an unease.

18

JAMAL WAS STANDING IN THE MOSQUE, HIS SHIRT AND kaili crumpled. Siddique, who walked in hurriedly, put his hand on his shoulder and asked, 'Are you well, maaple?'

Taken aback by the sudden movement, Jamal spun around to see who it was. Seeing Siddique there, his expression relaxed and he replied calmly, 'I am well. When did you come back from Tirupur?'

'Just today. In time for the Kandhuri festival at the mosque beginning tomorrow. Why are your kaili and shirt so wrinkled?'

'Pch, I had to go to Madurai for some work. I came straight to the mosque for the *asar* prayer, that's why.'

The two made their way towards the *avul* to perform olu. They found that the water in the tank was overflowing. 'What is the *mothinar* doing – why hasn't he turned off the motor?' Siddique said, looking around. He noticed Rasangam walking towards the motor switch and gathered that he was going to turn it off. 'Look at this man, strutting about in his sparkling white clothes,' he murmured to Jamal while shooting a pointed glance at Rasangam.

To Rasangam, who was now walking towards them, Siddique said, 'Did you turn off the switch? No matter what, only those who have known deprivation in their lives can truly understand the value of money. Did you notice how no one else here even realized the water was going to waste?'

Rasangam grew livid. Seething, he was determined to respond with something that would knock the wind out of them. 'Did any of us bring money along when we were born? Or are we going to take any with us when we die? It is His decree that everyone is entitled to only six feet in the kabristan,' he replied in a lowered voice and proceeded to perform olu.

'It's no big deal quoting a hadithu, maaple … you have to believe and strengthen the eemaan; live by it. Look at you, you don't even keep a beard,' Siddique said, stroking his own.

Rasangam stopped for a moment, straightened up and looked directly at them. 'People who talk ill of someone behind their back are bad people. The Rasul said this. No lineage outweighs the worth of good conduct. This, too, came from him,' his voice rang clear and deep.

There was no response from Siddique.

By then, Rasangam had finished his olu. For somebody who had come to the mosque just to be able to pray in peace, his mind was now tormented with frustration. *Did I cause any harm to anyone? Have my actions troubled others? Is their malice really just jealousy*? All these years, he had been observing how everyone gossiped about him and his inferior status behind his back, while ensuring he was able to overhear them.

What must I do to earn their respect? he wondered. He had already shown them that he had earned many more times the money he needed. Even after lavishly spending it on all kinds of shows of luxury, like buying a car and a bike, he couldn't understand the reason behind the persistent sense of disparity between him and the others in the village. *What pride do they find in doing all this?* His mind wilted.

'Allah … it is in Your name that I offer this sabur,' he said, commencing his prayers.

19

FATHIMA AND RASIYA WERE HEADING TOWARDS THE river. Darkness still lingered on their path. The occasional croaking of frogs and chirping of birds were captivating. The fragrance of the herbal shrubs along with the odour of damp coconut fiber drifting on the breeze gently eased the stress of Rasiya's mind.

Shameema walked ahead of them. The pleasant breeze felt soothing. The spring in the child's stride was delightful to watch even in the darkness. *Why can't I stop thinking about amma always fretting over how quickly she's growing up? Where has the father of this child run off to?* Frustrated, Fathima forced spit from the depths of her belly. In the dim glow of the streetlights, the irritation on her face stood out.

'You seem preoccupied …' Rasiya said.

'Just mulling over my fate. I wonder when Shameema is going to hit puberty …' Fathima replied softly. She was cautious to keep her child from overhearing her.

'Then who am I to rant to about my naseeb?' Rasiya whispered. The suffering in her words was beyond anyone's comprehension, Fathima realized and walked in silence. Their strides were perfectly in sync, their feet moving in the same direction.

Hanifa was behaving normally these days. Still, at night, unable to bear his violent intimacy, Rasiya would flee her room, sobbing, and take refuge in Fathima's. 'He is not okay. I will not even lie next to him from now on,' Fathima remembered her crying.

When it was decided that Rasiya would be Hanifa's bride, Fathima recalled her amma saying, 'She's such a beauty! Such a pious girl – Allah has blessed a family too poor to afford a square meal with a daughter of such divine beauty.' A great sadness gripped Fathima's heart. *Just how patient Rasiya is! In spite of all that has happened, she has not abandoned the family.* She was stunned by Rasiya's ability to contain her anger and not unleash it on anyone.

Over time, her pity for Rasiya had turned into an immeasurable love. *Is it really just compassion that turns into love? Though these urges have become rarer now – and that is for the better – when they do appear, I struggle to contain them. Bodily urges drain the life from me as I lay awake through countless nights. How time has slipped while I ponder ways to silence them.*

A sigh escaped Fathima. The waves rippling from the gentle caress of the breeze stirred her in an inexplicable way. The pebbles sparkled in the clear waters.

'Amma!' Shameema ran towards Fathima and wrapped her arms tightly around her waist.

'It is not cold at all, isn't it!' Rasiya teased Shameema.

'Maami is lying,' the child whined.

'It will be cold, but won't you still bathe, my sweet little girl?' Rasiya said. She scooped up water using her cupped palms and splashed it on the child's face, laughing. Endless laughter ensued, spilling onto the waves and spreading across the shores.

Fathima joined in, wanting to partake in the boundless laughter. The sound of their merriment gushed out like water released after years of confinement.

20

THE RACKET BANU CREATED WHILE WAKING HER SON up for school shook the whole house. 'Saniyan, you're going to be in *balaamusibath* for not waking up in the morning!'

Rasangam's temper shot through the roof as he sat trying to read the newspaper. *Doesn't she ever have anything nice to say to the child?* he thought to himself but said nothing. Not that she would have let him open his mouth at all. 'Cantankerous woman,' he murmured quietly. Since Asik machaan had died, Aabida's voice had waned. The guilt from failing to prevent his death had been eating away at Rasangam, too.

The two men had got ready in the morning and left for the shop as usual that Friday. Around noon, Asik had said, 'I feel a little weird … I will go home to take rest for some time and come back later for *joomma*,' and got ready to leave. Rasangam had dropped him home on his motorcycle.

He had never said anything of the sort before. His well-built body had been shaking as if from weakness; his face, red and sweaty.

'Aabida, bring some buttermilk for machaan,' Rasangam had sat Asik down and turned on the fan. The courtyard was burning in the fierce afternoon heat.

'I'll be right there!' As Aabida had begun churning some buttermilk, Banu had filled up a flask and brought it over. By then, Asik's face and clothes had been completely soaked in sweat.

Banu had hurriedly grabbed a Kutralam towel from the almirah and wiped his face, asking, 'How are you feeling, anne?' There was fear in her voice.

'I … just feel faint … I didn't sleep well last night …' he had replied.

'Here, drink some buttermilk,' Aabida had said, putting the tumbler to his lips and helping him drink. By then, Savura and Aamina from next door and Rasaaq from the shop had all gathered in their house.

'How are you feeling? Have you had enough to eat since the morning?' Asik's kuppi, Aamina, had asked with concern, sitting by the headboard of his bed.

Asik's face had darkened with fear.

When Rasangam had called the doctor, the nurse had replied saying, 'Sorry, sir has left for the General Hospital in a neighbouring village.' He had put down the receiver feeling betrayed. Asik's body had continued to be drenched in sweat.

'What did you give him to eat this morning?' Aamina kuppi had asked Aabida.

'Green bean kuzhambu and idli,' she had replied.

'It must be gas that's troubling the poor child so much. Bring me some milk boiled with garlic,' Aamina had said.

Rasangam had urged them, 'No, let's go to the hospital in Madurai, I will get the car.' He had been shaking with panic.

The call for *paangu* prayer quietened everyone for a few moments.

'It is time for joomma. Let's offer our prayers before we leave,' Aamina's husband Sabibullah had declared.

'We can't wait until then. We can do the joomma after consulting with the doctor in Madurai. Aabida, pack two saris and blouses in the yellow cloth bag and let's go,' Rasangam had insisted.

Rasangam's commanding tone had angered Sabibullah. 'What did I say and what are you doing? How can we cross the threshold of our village without performing joomma? Or do you think we can do joomma whenever we feel like it? Do you even know anything about eemaan?' he had yelled.

Rasaaq had said, 'Yes, let's wind up joomma and leave in an hour. Calm down – what is the rush?'

Asik's family had seemed adamant on putting an end to Rasangam's urgency. Finally, Asik weighed in, 'Let's finish with our prayers and then leave. Don't worry, I'm sure it's nothing.'

They finally left only after they had finished offering their jumu'ah prayers and Asik had died halfway to the hospital.

'If you had brought him as soon as he had started complaining, we could have saved him. You seem to have taken your own sweet time getting him here,' the doctor had said. His words made Rasangam break into sobs.

Aabida had stood frozen, unable to comprehend what had happened. Her life had more or less come to an end. If only she had known to leave two hours earlier and fend off his relatives, who had hindered her from making the right decision in that moment ... She had been completely broken.

Rasangam often wondered if he should send Imran someplace faraway for his education. If he put him in a good convent school, he could study well, unaffected by the goings-on of the village and the annoying habits of his mother. But he did not know how to broach the subject with Banu.

'I can't send him away as if he were an orphan! Do you want to kill him by putting him into a hostel without access to good, homecooked meals?'

She believed that to come from a well-off family meant teaching one's children about the power of money and living lavishly. 'That's how we have lived for generations,' she would argue and it was impossible to change her mind about it. She said this from time to time just to feel satisfied with putting her husband in his place.

For a while now, he had become indifferent to her behaviour, dismissing it as mere ignorance or immaturity.

Since Aabida was required by custom to leave home to mark the completion of the *Iddah* period, Rasangam and she had decided to pay their mother a visit that day.

'Why don't I just live with them? It's not as if I have a child or anything there,' Aabida had said. The weight of the sorrow in her voice had been too much for Rasangam to bear; he had sunk, feeling defeated.

'Then, should I return to live there by myself? With Banu?' The questions had almost rolled off the tip of his tongue, but he had remained silent, not wanting to worry his mother or anyone else at home. Later, he had said to her, 'Come with me, there is so much work to take care of there. Imran will also ask for his kuppi.'

Mahamooda and Sainambu had looked on as if they had discerned something unsaid, but they couldn't be sure. Either way, there hadn't been room for such speculation. Fathima's mind had been somewhere else, even as she had been combing Shameema's hair. It had been clear that she had merely been pretending to be fully immersed in the activity. Rasiya had sat with her gaze fixed on the courtyard, indifferent to everything around her. Hanifa had been asleep inside his room.

When the cows and chicken had begun to return to their shed, Fathima had sprang up and hurried out. The sound of the paangu call for the *maghrib* prayers had filled the air.

'I don't know whose curse has befallen us – the lives of our daughters have been completely ruined. I thought only our lives were a lost cause … yah Allah …' Mahamooda had lamented softly.

Hanifa had woken up and come out to sit on the pyol quietly. After a little while, he had said, 'Thambi, when did you arrive? Aabida, how are you, my darling?' His lifeless voice had further pained Rasangam; he had thrown both his arms around his brother and hugged him tightly. Tears had streamed down his face. Hanifa's body had become frail.

As Aabida and Rasangam had sat in the car and got ready to leave, they had heard someone stifling their sobs with the loose end of a sari. He had started driving, wondering anxiously if it had been only one of them or all four.

'Here I am struggling with this child all by myself! Look at you sitting there like a rock,' Banu's voice brought Rasangam back to the present.

'Leave the child with me. I will drop him to school,' he said.

'Keep your bullshit help to yourself. I'll handle it.'

He looked at her for a second with disgust, then ground his teeth to control his anger. He reminded himself how she never spoke so crudely. He calmed himself down, went into his room, put on a cassette tape and played a song. He wondered if Ilayaraja's music could soothe his troubled mind. It had become impossible for him to fully immerse himself in music lately.

When it didn't work, he picked up the phone to call his mother.

'Hanifa doesn't eat properly these days, da. He's become so thin. He sleeps only on the pyol. The girl goes into the room quietly by herself every night,' his amma and sachaani took turns crying and blowing their noses into their saris.

'I have consulted a doctor. We'll get him admitted into the hospital in Madurai this week,' he said, trying to comfort them. When it turned out to be too hard, he put down the receiver with a heavy heart.

When he had gone to Madurai for collecting dues, his supplier Basheer had said, 'Dr Khan, who lives here, is a really good psychiatrist. Why don't you take your brother to him?'

His only concern pertained to the village that he lived in catching wind of it. As things stood, Banu's family hardly respected him. If they came to know his brother needed a psychiatrist, they would torment him even more.

'Basheer bhai, please don't breathe a word of this to anyone from my village – not even my family or any of the other suppliers. If the village comes to know, they will harass me no end.'

Taking pity on his pleading voice, Basheer patted him on his shoulder supportively. 'Don't worry about all that. Allah is enough.'

He got the contact information for Dr Khan from him. He resolved not to let Banu find out. She may bring it up in front of her relatives in casual conversation. Moreover, the next time she yelled at him, she would throw Hanifa's illness in his face.

21

WHEN HE LEFT THAT MORNING, RASANGAM INFORMED Banu that he was going to Madurai for work. He did not say anything to Aabida either. She was in the backyard with Maimoona, cooking the batter they had ground in a pot to make vadakams. He did not want to say anything in front of their domestic help, so he simply left without a word.

It was this kind of work that Aabida took upon herself when she had spare time. She made a whole year's worth of vadakam, appalam, vatthal, flour to make idiyaapams, sun-dried salted meat and so on. She took Maimoona's help in making the preparations. Their relationship was quite amazing. Maimoona, too, had lost her husband. She had two daughters. She would often say, 'I came here to this village with just the shirt on my back and my two girls – with not even the means to get my next meal. It is this magnanimous family that graciously took me in.'

Rasangam's mind was in distress. *I don't feel good about hiding from Banu that I'm going to see my mother and then admit Hanifa in a hospital for psychiatric treatment. If not today then one of these days, the news will reach her through someone else from the village anyway. When that happens, she will get very angry and twist things out of proportion. It'll certainly be very difficult to calm her down then* … His mind continued to race in confusion as he headed towards his village.

He crossed the main road and turned onto the road leading to his village. The first coconut grove at the entrance to the village had been the one Hanifa had taken on lease for a few years. The last time he had visited home, he had asked his amma, who had leased it now. 'It's the village revenue officer. The grove owner came by the other day and complained to me that it's no longer the same as when we were managing it. Apparently, the officer's wife is very stingy with the coconuts,' he recalled her saying.

Those trees had been in their care for so many years. Hanifa had looked after them like his own. Often, Rasangam would accompany him on his bicycle to go check on the trees or oversee the pruning of the branches. It was only a kilometre away from their village. They would drink the tender coconut water that Chinnaiyya would rush to bring them and chat about the latest movie playing at the theatre or about actors and actresses. They would discuss in great detail the clothes that the actors wore. Even though they both put in effort into their appearances and wanted to look good, Hanifa was a lot more particular. Once, after watching a Rajesh Khanna movie, he had shaved off his moustache and got an earful from Rasangam's amma for it.

'What is this look – a spineless cactus?' she had said and chased after him with a broom. The recollection of how his sachaani had laughed hard enjoying the show, sitting on the paddy-pounding mortar, brought tears to his eyes. Noticing them rolling down his face, he pulled the car over to the side.

There was a tiny bridge over the flowing river. Even though the current was not very strong, the fresh, chlorophyllic smell of the plants, the ripples on the surface of the water and the calls of the birds mesmerized his senses. He got out of his car to try and regain his composure. The tranquility of the environment calmed his racing mind. The tap-tapping of the woodpeckers, the cooing of the cuckoos made his heart feel lighter. He watched a flock of sparrows pecking amidst the shrubs. Their little chirps were pleasing to the ears. *I am a father to a son. Why am I standing here with tears in my eyes like I am still a child?* he chided himself and wiped his eyes with his handkerchief. With so much responsibility on his shoulders, he couldn't afford to tear up in self-pity this way. He wondered what state their house was in. *I don't know what state of mind amma, sachaani and Rasiya will be in. Please grant me the mental strength to overcome it all, Allah*, he prayed and started the car.

'Why you do kill yourself over your sachaani's family, I don't understand. Nowhere else in the world would anyone spend the kind of money you do on them or run around for them like you do,' Banu would carp once in a while.

Amma was sitting on the pyol. Sachaani was nowhere to be seen. As usual, Fathima came out of the kitchen. 'Come, attha,' his amma said.

'Where is anna? I don't see him,' he asked her.

She pointed to his room, then said, 'Sit down, attha ...'

He handed Fathima the bag he had brought along. It had fruits and biscuits he had bought for Shameema. She must have been at school at the time.

He did not enquire about Rasiya. Distinct were the pangs of his heart when he thought about her. Why should her life have to turn out this way just because she came from a poor family? As his mind started fretting over why no one's life in his house had turned out happy, he stopped himself short of spiralling into self-pity again and turned his thoughts to God. *Allah is enough.*

Hanifa was curled up sleeping. 'Anne, wake up. Look who has come.'

Hearing Rasangam's voice, Hanifa opened his eyes and sat up immediately. 'Thambi, when did you arrive?' His question was enthusiastic, but his voice was breaking. His face was sunken. Seeing him in a crumpled shirt and kaili with his entire appearance completely altered was unbearable. The image of Hanifa trying to look like Rajesh Khanna without his moustache momentarily flashed in front of Rasangam's eyes.

He clenched his jaw to control his tears and took his brother in his arms. 'Salaam alaykum, anne! How are you doing? Usually, you are the one to wish me first. Why didn't you?' he asked. 'Salaam alaykum, salaam alaykum, thambi. I forgot. When did you come and how are you doing? Why have you lost weight?'

'No anne, I'm doing just fine. Okay, get up now, let's get you bathed. We will go into town after we eat,' he replied, holding his hand and helping him stand up.

Rasiya was standing on one side. Even though he felt rather awkward looking directly at her, he had to acknowledge her presence. 'Salaam, machi,' he said. Her face brightened like the moon in response. He was so enraptured that he momentarily lost control. Those clear, grief-soaked eyes bewildered him with their alluring beauty. He peeled his eyes away and hurried Hanifa out of their room.

Amma had already shut the front door preemptively, lest neighbours and relatives came rushing in hearing Rasangam's car pull in. Because Rasangam gave them money every time he came home, they flocked eagerly to see him. But no one wanted them there today. Sachaani emerged from the cowshed and then went back in to feed the calf water with bran mixed in. That's when she saw Rasangam. 'Come, attha,' she called out. Turning to Hanifa, she said, 'Hanifa, please bathe, attha.' Her voile sari was soaked and had bits of bran stuck to it. She herded the calf away from the bran water pot towards the water trough.

Content with having his brother by his side, Hanifa went to the well to take a bath without any resistance.

'I have asked Ajmal to come to the hospital. Sachaani, you and Hanifa can stay in the hospital itself. Ajmal will be there with you for support. Just one week should be enough,' Rasangam informed Mahamooda.

When they got into the car, Hanifa didn't say a word. He did not ask where they were going.

Bidding goodbye to his mother and sister, Rasangam's eyes once again fell on Rasiya's face. With effort, he tore his gaze away from her and started his car. He noticed that her lips were twitching as if she wished to say something.

The hospital was located in Tallakulam. It was an old two-storeyed building at the end of a narrow lane. They saw a lady there, sitting on a chair scribbling something in a notebook. She made for a pitiful sight in her emaciated body and protruding teeth.

Dr Khan examined Hanifa and said, 'I have never seen a patient be so cooperative before. Let him stay here for a week. We will put him on a course of medication and counselling. After that, medicines alone should do and he can go home. Don't worry.' His reassuring words made Rasangam feel lighter.

'I will come back tomorrow. Take good care of yourself,' he said, hugging and kissing Hanifa. He placed a bundle of cash in his sachaani's hands. 'Take care of him,' he said and left.

'You go home. I'll be careful,' Hanifa sent off his little cousin with a smile on his tired face.

An insufferable sadness swept over him. It had started raining outside. 'Drive carefully,' Hanifa's words rang in his ears. He got into his car and left.

22

'IF YOU HAD TOLD ME YOU WERE GOING TO MADURAI yesterday, I would also have come with you,' Banu said.

'I did tell you, though. You should have come along then,' Rasangam said as he sat down in his chair. 'What's for dinner?'

'I had soaked rice to make rice vathal. How could I just have come along? Although if I had, I would have been able to buy some saris and fabric. Everything's always such a secret,' she complained. 'Idli and meat broth,' she said and served him some idlis. 'You could have got Amsavalli biryani from Madurai. You know I like it. But it doesn't even occur to you, does it? So useless!'

'Are you going to let me eat or not? Complaining all the time,' he raised his voice slightly. He just wanted to peacefully listen to the song playing on his tape recorder. Her constant grumbling irritated him.

'You never like it when I say anything. Okay, I will just leave then,' she said, making her way to the kitchen.

'Thank God!' Rasangam sighed in relief. If he was going to Madurai, she had to come with him. She had to buy piles of saris and jewellery. It was almost a sort of mental sickness. *But we have the money so what is wrong in her wanting to enjoy all that?* he reasoned, *Banu is not a bad person.* She was inclined to helping others and was sensitive to their pain. She could still sometimes behave foolishly or pettily and at those times, he would deliberately ignore her lest there be any quarrels.

The cassette tape continued playing, but he couldn't enjoy it. The doctor's words did comfort him and helped him feel a little more confident, yet he couldn't help feeling concerned about how his sachaani and Ajmal were managing and whether Hanifa was behaving himself. If he called to check on them, Banu would come to know. *If not right away, then in another day or so. Someone from the village will definitely tell her.* He felt exhausted thinking about all that.

Wondering how he could make a call without her finding out, he called out, 'Aabida?'

'What is it, anne?' she said, walking over to him.

'You are in the house, aren't you? Why are you still wearing your headscarf – aren't you feeling hot?' he asked with concern.

Banu prayed five times a day. Aabida prayed nine times. She fasted every week and never took her headscarf off. She seemed to have found her home in the belief that God was enough.

'No, I'm not sweating,' she replied and then asked him, 'Have you eaten? When did you get back from Madurai?'

'I came back in the evening. Has the child slept? I couldn't even get anything back for him.'

Sensing that he wanted to say more but was hesitating, her gaze travelled towards the kitchen. She saw Banu standing there. The siblings remained quiet.

'The two of us have been very busy since the morning. We made vadagam today, you see. We had to grind the rice, steam the flour, squeeze it through the press ... Going up and down the steps to the terrace really hurts my legs. My hip hurts too. That's why I laid my bed out early,' Aabida chattered on just for the sake of filling the silence.

'Yes, I'm also feeling really tired. Here, drink this milk,' Banu placed a cup of milk on the table.

'Okay, you both go to bed. So will I, in a bit.' Rasangam sent them away and sipped on the milk.

Right after he woke up in the morning, he called Ajmal once Aabida got busy in the kitchen and Banu was focused on getting their son ready for school. Once Sachaani said, 'everything is alright,' he felt relieved. He left to open the shop for the day.

The doctor had mentioned that he himself would call him after the first session of counselling. He called him around noon and said, 'There's nothing to worry about. He is alright, he was cooperative. We can bring him back.' Hearing this, Rasangam felt his heart float on the breeze.

He immediately called amma and Rasiya, wanting to share the news. It was Rasiya who answered the phone. When he heard her voice, he went quiet for a little bit before greeting her with a salaam. 'The doctor says there's nothing to worry about,' he told her.

'Salaam, machaan. Oh, okay machaan, amma has just stepped out. I'll let her know. I am putting all my trust in you.' Her voice made him uncomfortable. Unable to tell whether he felt saddened or intoxicated by it, he stammered. Her face and eyes flashed in his mind and tormented him. The doubt if it was sympathy he felt for her or something else froze him in place. Why did her beauty tantalize him so? The cruelty of her having to spend her life with someone who did not value her beauty and of Hanifa's condition gnawed at him.

Unable to say anything more, he hung up. Although he knew she would still be holding the receiver at the other end, he worried that if he continued to talk, he might perturb her. *Everything will be alright in a few months.* He was hopeful that once Hanifa was cured, he would be able to talk to Rasiya without any sense of guilt or turmoil. Feeling spirited, he started his work. The store saw a lot of business that day. He sat at the cash register constantly and could not even find time to have his lunch. Banu had called twice already. Why did he feel so contented? He was optimistic that since he needn't worry too much about Hanifa anymore, he could focus on his work peacefully from now on.

23

AS HE PREPARED TO LEAVE FOR HOME AT SEVEN THAT evening, Rasangam realized that he had only had tea all day. He summoned the shop boy and sent him to Royal restaurant to buy parotta and egg kalaki for him. He could have gone over to eat there itself, but had he done so, he would have been engaged by at least a couple of relatives in pointless conversation. They would either enquire after Hanifa or remark at how he chose to drive to the restaurant even though it was only a few shops away just to brandish his affluence. He wanted to avoid all that.

After eating, he must go for the *isha* prayer. Today, he had missed the maghrib prayer. He had offered the *dhuhr* and asr prayers upstairs.

Rasaaq returned and served the parottas upstairs, bidding him to eat. Just then, the telephone rang. He picked up, thinking it must be Banu. It was his sachaani.

'Rasangam, we can't find Hanifa! I am doomed!' She said and started wailing loudly over the phone.

Her voice and words struck him on the head like a lightning bolt. 'What happened … how did it happen?

I'm coming right away, please don't cry,' he responded in a panic. He quickly put the phone down and hurried to close the shop. Seeing him panicked, Rasaaq quickly switched off all the lights and helped pull down the shutter.

'I am leaving for Madurai. Hand over the keys to the shop to Banu,' he said and ran to his car parked in an open space behind the shop. It started raining just as he set off. *Where could Hanifa have gone! He must be getting soaked in this rain!* He drove on, cursing the rain.

'How could you have admitted him to a hospital without even telling your own wife? Would I have bitten your head off over something like that?' Banu complained. 'Why does a man who prays five times a day need lies?' she grumbled on, shoving his pain aside. Rasangam paid no attention to her. Imran sat next to his attha, quietly observing everything. Aabida was sitting in an inner room, sniffling.

He had filed a complaint with the police. Notices were printed and posted on every street corner in Madurai. A week had passed. He too had grown weary of looking for Hanifa at their usual spots. He didn't have the courage to face Rasiya. Even though he had reassured her when they had spoken over the phone, he had lost all hope himself.

'He was doing just fine! He asked to be taken to watch a movie. You know how much he likes movies. That's why we went. He bought the tickets. He had dressed up like a groom in a shirt and veshti, his hair combed back and he had even dusted on some talcum powder. Because I was with him, I wasn't too worried about making the trip. During the interval, my boy said he needed to use the restroom. I stood outside waiting for him to come out but he never did!' Sachaani had said, crying her heart out.

'Will you *please* shut up?! Your incessant complaining is giving me a headache!' he shouted with irritation. No one had ever heard him raise his voice that high. Banu too felt a little fearful for the first time. She looked at him closely, as if to ask, 'why are you so angry?'

As someone who understood his anger, to an extent, Aabida actually welcomed it. It was not only directed at Banu but also himself. It was an explosion triggered by his inability to bear the contemptuous comments and mockery by the whole village over Hanifa's disappearance. *Good. If he continued to keep that bottled up, it would be harmful for his heart. Letting it all out is the right thing to do*, she soothed her mind.

Rasangam spent driving around from town to town in his car looking for Hanifa for at least two days every week. Every time he set out to look for him, Aabida would promise an oblation to Goddess Arakaasamman and await his return.

24

A WEEK AFTER HANIFA WENT MISSING, RASANGAM WAS taken by surprise when Rasiya called him one day to seek his permission for moving back to her parents' house.

'Why, what happened?' he said, bewildered, unable to say more.

'Aabida akka mentioned that Banu lambasts you at home every time you come here. That's why ...' Her voice sounded distant.

'No, no, it's not like Banu is suspicious of me or anything. It might just have been Aabida's imagination.'

'Well, I too find my heart faltering and that's not good. That's why I want to go back to my house, machaan.'

Neither had anything more left to say beyond that. Her voice trembled as she hung up the phone. *With such ease, the woman has expressed her desire; why can't I get myself to say those words and share my feelings?*

The moment stretched on for several minutes as the two of them remained deeply absorbed in their thoughts. They worried about how they were going to go on with their lives after that moment.

'How can I stop her from going when she has made

up her mind? It is her dumb, good-for-nothing mother who is not letting her stay here. There is no food in their house – what is she going to do there? Are they all going to starve together?' his amma and sachaani griped on and on.

'From now on, I will send you money every month. You can give it to Rasiya,' he said to calm them down.

Fathima's heart was drowned in endless grief and loneliness. She had only just found someone like herself to be by her side at all times. Just the thought of being left alone in her stifling room after Rasiya was gone made her feel distraught. She prayed five times a day and spent most of her time begging Allah to help them find Hanifa annan somehow.

Whenever Rasangam ventured out in his car, he hoped, as he scanned the streets, to spot Hanifa standing somewhere. At times, if he spotted someone half-clad and unstable, he would pull over and rush over to them to check if it was him, only to be disappointed. Whenever he ate good food or watched a movie at the cinema theatre, he could not help but think of Hanifa. He was constantly plagued by anxiety about where he must be wandering, hungry and alone.

'This year, I would like to provide kanji during the fast, in my name as a representative of my family,' Rasangam said to the muttawalli, the manager of the mosque. At the time, no one else was around in the mosque's inner courtyard. Yasinbhai looked at his face closely. 'My mind is constantly anxious; I can't find inner peace. I will sponsor the kanji. I will contribute one lakh towards the expansion of the mosque. I will also contribute to the mosque's *kumaru* fund to help with the wedding expenses of girls from impoverished families,' he added.

The muttawalli looked closely at him. *He looks like he will say yes to anything I ask for*, he thought, *And it won't be for nothing – he would have the good fortune of providing the kanji*. 'Aren't you doing that already under your Asik machaan's name? You are the one paying for it. Then why more?' he asked.

'Yes, but that is not in my name.'

'So what if it isn't? Well … if anyone in the village acquiesces their turn to provide kanji, I will put your name down.'

'Can you change Asik machaan's turn to mine then?' he asked before taking his leave. 'I have to go now, I'll see you later.'

As Rasangam walked away, the muttawalli called after him, 'Contribute what you can towards construction work.'

Sponsoring porridge during the month of fasting was an honour bestowed upon one in their village. His attempt to somehow buy that honour for himself did not pan out as he had intended. He felt very frustrated. His mind sprinted at a dizzying pace to figure out what he could do to make the people of this village come crawling to him.

The day before, Banu's once-removed uncle Salil had hosted a function in honour of their grandson's circumcision and invited half the village for a feast. Aabida had asked Banu, 'Why didn't they invite Rasangam?'

'I don't know ... Apparently, they only invited close male relatives. They could have invited my husband, too. They are just a jealous bunch. Those who flocked to eat there must be desperate for food. They all claim to have glorious lineages and mighty titles. But none of them have anything to show for it. Yet, they want to make a show of excluding him from all of it, those jealous mongrels!' Banu had ranted in a single breath.

After the dhuhr prayer ended, Rasangam noticed that instead of leaving one by one as they usually did, people were leaving in groups of ten or twelve. He asked them, 'Where are you all off to together? Is there a feast somewhere?'

'Salil Rawther's family is hosting a feast for his grandson's *sunnah* – didn't they invite you?' Rasaaq had asked, sarcastically.

Realizing he may have walked into a trap unwittingly, he had replied, 'No, I didn't know. I'm just on my way out of town anyway,' trying to hide his disappointment.

'Where to? In search of your annan again? The one who went mad and then got lost? That one? You still have hope?' Yusuf had mocked him.

Rasangam had clenched his teeth and swallowed the flash of anger he had felt and performed sabr. 'Allah ...

you listen to all this.' His words got caught in his throat. With no intention to respond to them, he stood holding his palms facing up in supplication.

25

'YOUR BROTHER SENDS MONEY TO RASIYA EVERY MONTH, doesn't he?' Banu sounded annoyed.

'Yes, you know that already,' Aabida replied as she picked out the stones from the rice grains in a *kundani*, a large-bottomed vessel. 'So many stones,' she declared when she finished looking through it.

'Do you know what they say about that in our village?' Banu said, spreading out the slices of the brinjal she had just cut, inspecting the pieces for worms.

'This wretched village … Everyone says whatever they want. How are we to live if we pay heed to everything they have to say?' Aabida did not let those thorny words of ridicule break through.

'Then he shouldn't complain about how no one in the village respects him either, no?'

'First of all, who in this village is qualified to even respect Rasangam? Can they even measure up to the dust beneath his feet? What character, intelligence, talent, looks and merciful heart he has!' Aabida said and turned around to spit in the courtyard.

'So what if one has money? Who cares about that? It has to do with us and our family and whether or not we live an honourable life – that is what they will talk about,' Banu said with a barb.

'Why, what is dishonourable about my family? A person suffering from mental illness – is that so shameful? It isn't as if our entire family has mental issues. Will Allah not present anyone in this village with any problems? The men and women here talk as if they've forgotten all about the existence of Allah and now you parrot them?' Aabida lashed out.

Banu was startled; she had never heard Aabida speak with such aggression until then. Aabida was furious. Her face was flushed with rage and dripping with sweat; her body was trembling, wrapped in her chiffon saree.

'Please stay calm, don't get angry. Here, drink some water,' Banu quickly got up and grabbed a water sombu. She held Aabida in her arms and made her take a sip.

After taking a sip, Aabida staggered towards her room. Banu tried to support her, but she shrugged off her hands. She walked into her room by herself and lay down on her bed.

Fathima's runaway husband, the disappearance of Hanifa, Rasiya's darkened face, Asik's death – everything came crashing down on her all at once and left her in tears. Sobbing softly, she tried to push past the deep, years' worth of sorrow. But none of it was going to be washed away with her tears or easily forgotten. She found herself drifting deeper into a pit, struggling to find a way to rise above the self-pity that had reduced her to tears.

26

'YOU WANT TO DO *HAJ*? AT YOUR AGE? STOP MESSING about,' Banu thought that Rasangam was joking.

'Yes, I've applied for it. Is this a matter to be joking about?' he gently admonished his wife. Imran, who was writing something in a notebook, looked up at his father.

'Your son is only eight years old. Also, if you leave so suddenly, who will take care of the store? Doesn't Allah say that all duties must be completed before proceeding on Haj?'

'Ajmal will take care of the store. He has already completed his Pre-University. I don't have any debts to pay off. So why not?'

'After you return from Haj, you, sir, cannot enjoy movies or music, or dress up stylishly like you do. You must live an austere life like a Sufi saint – you know that don't you?' she said and laughed teasingly.

'Of course, what makes you think I don't? Silly woman … you think I can't live without cinema and music?' Rasangam laughed.

'Attha, what is Haj? Where are you going?' Imran asked eagerly.

'Attha will be going to a foreign country in an aeroplane. I will bring back chocolates, sweets, toy cars and more for you.' He sat his son on his lap, hugged and kissed him.

Banu showed no sign of happiness. 'My attha went for Haj at the age of fifty-five. Why do you want to go now, when you are not even thirty? Sure, Ajmal may be your younger brother, but entrusting the business to him doesn't sound like a good idea.'

Rasangam smiled faintly. 'Nothing of that sort will happen. I am only putting my trust in Allah. He will take care of everything; you just be brave. Allah likes those who seek *ilmu* at younger age. He won't leave us in want of anything. He will make sure the business runs smoothly.'

Banu observed her husband's face intently. She believed that Allah, who had blessed her with such a dignified and virtuous husband would certainly not leave her needs unfulfilled. She decided to let go of unnecessary fears. Her mind became absorbed in calculating how many sovereigns' worth of gold jewellery and what kinds of pieces she ought to have him bring back for her when he returned. Knowing exactly what was on her mind in that moment, Rasangam shed any concerns he had about her. She had an inherent innocence to her. That was also why his love for her knew no bounds. Petty, materialistic things were enough for her to be happy.

As far as he was concerned, he had no loans; only

duties to take care of. It was his responsibility to get Fathima's daughter Shameema married. Looking for a groom outside their village was not an option because the girl's father was not in the picture. He had arranged for her to be wedded to Abubaker, who owned a chili depot in the same village. The groom had consented without harbouring any expectations from the family. Rasangam really appreciated that about him. He decided he would build a small house behind amma and sachaani's house for Fathima so she could live out her life there peacefully.

Rasangam had already bought a warehouse close to the village market in Shameema's name for her groom to permanently run his chili business from. He had also booked a Bullet motorbike for him, which he could use to travel to the neighbouring villages to buy stock conveniently. He planned to organize for their nikkah after his return from Haj. Abubaker had great respect and love for Rasangam for not only finding him a bride, but for also planning for his future so meticulously.

For Rasiya, he gave his sachaani a lakh to open a fixed deposit under her name, but she refused it, with tears in her eyes. For Ajmal, too, to strengthen his sense of responsibility, he bid him to come and look after his store.

A strong urge arose within him to spend the rest of his days practicing *amal*, doing good deeds and staying true to his religious beliefs so he may free himself from the anguish and shame he endured pursuing honour and prestige. Even though he was not entirely free of self-doubt, uncertain whether his hopes were achievable and his choices right, that was what he wanted for himself. Without seeking God, there was no way he could have accumulated such wealth. He wished to do his part and express his gratitude by being altruistic. For the benefit of the people of the village, who had slighted him at every turn, mocked his brother Hanifa's condition and laughed derisively at his family background, he wished to create a new self-identity which would inspire them to give him the respect that he deserved – and much more – of their own accord.

I will have to give up some indulgences as collateral against my dreams. He sensed the neatly arranged rows of Tamil movie song cassette tapes in his almirah mock him. *Banu, Ajmal, Imran … perhaps one of them might like to have these. Once I return from Haj, I will have to distance myself from the measly pleasures of this dunya, this material world.*

Aabida was sad. She knew all too well her elder brother's innate zest for life. He'd watch every movie as soon as it was released, come home to talk about it and act it out, dressing up like the actors and styling his hair like theirs, getting scolded by their amma for it, listening to songs from the movies and then singing them. For someone who had grown up seeing him flitting about like a colourful butterfly only to give it all up so suddenly like a *Haji*, renouncing all desires at such a young age, appeared rather excessive.

'Life unfolds in phases. One must do the things appropriate for their age – that's how it is meant to be,' sachaani and amma's words echoed in Aabida's ears. She smiled imagining how sachaani would react to the news of Rasangam doing the Haj. 'Ada, clueless juveniles, no point talking sense to you,' and with that, sachaani would dismiss the conversation.

If Hanifa and Rasangam wanted to go to a movie every week, she was the one who gave them the money for it. As soon as they came back, she would ask them all about it. She would be so lost listening to all the details they shared with her that she would even forget that they were her children.

Aabida also wanted to undertake Haj. She did not have any duties to fret over, either. After Asik's demise, she didn't have much of a desire for anything. Once, when Rasangam had asked his little sister if she would like anything, she had dismissed the intent behind his question. The jewels Asik had got made for her over the years, the wealth and property he had accumulated were more than enough to take care of her needs. 'You don't worry about me. From now on, my only needs are food and seeking ilmu,' she had told him.

Next time, when Banu goes for Haj is when I can go along too, she decided as she got up to perform olu. In the distance, the call for prayer could be heard. This year, Rasangam had contributed funds for the construction of a new mosque on North Street. When the local chief, the mosque's muttawalli and the trustee were discussing the possibility of building a new mosque to create more space for the Friday prayers and accommodate the growing crowd, Rasangam was the first to stand up and declare the amount he was willing to donate to the cause, making jaws drop all around him. *Who in this village has the heart or the means to make such a donation?* Aabida laughed to herself.

27

A KILOMETRE AWAY FROM THE OUTSKIRTS OF THE village, a crowd led by the head of the village's Islamic council stood waiting to receive the village's first Haji. Getting out of his car, Rasangam looked like a Sufi saint in his white attire. His lean physique, light stubble and the white cloth cap covering his shaved head held everyone in thrall. The important people of the village came forward to greet him with salaams and embraces, complete with *musafaha* and placing their cheek against his. An exotic fragrance of attar that exuded from his clothes seemed to hold the whole venue in an embrace.

The group paraded towards the mosque. In front of the crowd walked the hazrats chanting baith along with Rasangam. Sitting in the car, Aabida watched the scene unfold; her eyes welled up. Imran, who was sitting next to her, kept staring at her in concern and confusion, not knowing what was going on. *It would take some time for the procession to cross the market street and reach the mosque. There, the* asarathus *may deliver a few sermons or* bayaan *before coming home.* Aabida decided to head home in the car.

Banu was offering her prayers at home. She was awaiting the return of her husband, having refused to join the others for the welcome reception. Everyone from Rasangam's village, including amma, sachaani and Fathima, had come home to receive him.

To Banu's eager 'How does he look?', Aabida replied, 'He looks well. He's become a little thinner. He must have kept busy with amal and not eaten properly.'

'My son has lost weight?' amma asked her daughter, concerned.

'How did they welcome him?' Fathima asked eagerly.

'How do I even begin to describe the glorious event? So many people holding shawls and garlands for him.' Her eyes sparkled as she shared the details with great pride. 'Amma, you should have seen it – I may have cast an evil eye myself!'

No one had ever heard such splendour emanate from Aabida's voice. Banu sat looking at her, stunned. 'Ya Allah, rabbe!' Amma and Sachaani held up the loose ends of their saris towards the sky with both hands and cried. Seeing tears of joy streaming down their faces for the first time in a very long time made Aabida giddy to the point of madness. She dropped down to sit with her back against a wall, stretched out her legs and said, 'Maimoona, bring me some water!'

Mahamooda dashed into the kitchen. She retrieved the ingredients she needed to ward off the evil eye from her dear child from the spice box and folded them into a piece of paper. 'Imran, run outside and bring me a little bit of dust off the street, da. Let's remove all evil eyes off your attha.'

The whole house was buoyant. Women gathered at the house. Banu, who had taken on the responsibility of serving the Zamzam water and dates her husband had brought along to all guests, was spinning around the entire place like a top.

'How was your journey? How hot was it there? How were the crowds? Were you staying close to the *Kaaba* or within walking distance from it? Did you find our local food there? How did you feel when you saw the Kaaba?'

With pride and love, Banu admired the sight of her husband replying to the volley of questions directed at him with joy and enthusiasm. *How softly, politely and patiently he speaks. How much knowledge he has accrued in such a brief time*, she observed in awe and then remembered that he had always been this way. By the time the crowd finally dispersed, and the house fell quiet, everyone was tired.

Rasangam had grown very thin. Once Maimoona left after she had swept and mopped the house, Mahamooda latched the door and set about trying to ward off the evil eye from her child.

'This is all *shirk*, superstition, not Islam – don't do all this. If you really want to remove evil eye, please read a *surah*,' he said, getting up and walking away dismissively.

No one in the house slept that night. They were all

engrossed in Rasangam's stories, clinging to his every word with their mouths wide open. He described in great detail the sights that had him awestruck – the structure of the Kaaba, the crowds, the beauty of the Madina mosque, the provisions made to keep the passage between the hills of Safa and Marwah cool where he performed Thongottam, jogging seven times back and forth, the stoning of the devil and so on.

Sainambu and Mahamooda sat hooked, gaping the whole time. It all sounded unbelievable to them. They marvelled at how their son, born in a tiny hamlet, had turned out to be so blessed as to have visited Mecca in an unknown faraway land and stepped on that fabled holy soil. As pride welled naturally within her for her son, Sainambu closed her eyes and gave thanks to Allah. Ajmal was sitting next to his brother and observing him closely. The fear of God already in his heart grew multifold.

'Apparently, there is no tax on the jewellery you buy on Haj?' Banu remarked, sounding annoyed.

'Women are allowed to wear any amount of jewellery, but you cannot buy and carry it in boxes,' Rasangam replied. 'Tell me what sort of jewellery you want, we can buy it here,' he wrapped his arms around his wife to pacify her. 'In any case, one has very limited time there. Should one spend it doing religious service or looking for a jewellery shop? You tell me.'

Limp in the embrace of her husband after a long

period of staying apart, Banu relented to his argument. Still, wearing jewellery from abroad and flaunting it in front of other women had its own pleasure. The disappointment of being denied that pleasure lingered.

28

AFTER HIS MORNING BATH, RASANGAM GRABBED HIS keys hanging from a nail on the wall. Ajmal, who had gone to the mosque in the morning, had not yet returned.

'What time does he usually open the store every day? He still hasn't come back – it's nine already,' he asked Banu.

'He goes only at ten, like he was going to an office,' Banu hurled a sharp response.

Not caring for her tone, he cut short the conversation saying, 'I'm going to open the store.' He told Aabida, 'I'm heading to the store' and she nodded in acknowledgement. Banu's response had felt harsh to her, too. She waited for Rasangam to leave. There was still no sign of Ajmal. She suddenly remembered that he attended the Tabligh Jamaat Mashora, a council for an Islamic missionary movement, on Tuesdays.

Why does he have to be so involved in religious activities at such a young age? she wondered. *Rasangam has reached a comfortable status in society. It is good that he is doing what he is. But why is this boy roaming around in a cap and* jibba?

She smelled something burning and guessed Banu must be cooking in the kitchen. Aabida got up and latched the front door for fear of their domestic help Maimoona or Ajmal barging in any minute. She needed to talk to Banu before that. She entered the kitchen and stood in front of her. 'Why did you say that?' Banu was looking down, washing rice and raised her head to look at Aabida defiantly. Her face clearly expressed her lack of remorse. The water in the pot to cook rice was boiling.

'Why, I only spoke the truth. What's wrong with that?' she replied.

'Did you really tell the truth? That on Tuesdays, he comes home after the Mashora? Even if he wanted the car keys to go out somewhere, you scorned him for it. Why did you have to lie about him too? He is also his brother.'

Aabida's voice was calm instead of stern. Instead of getting angry, she stood there patiently, waiting for Banu to answer. There was no provocation for Banu to get angry, either. She spoke emphatically, 'You're the one reading so much into it. I answered the question normally. Must have.' She noticed tears forming in Aabida's eyes. Unwilling to engage with her any further, she walked away towards the courtyard.

There was a knock on the door. Aabida wiped her tears and walked over to open it. 'Salaam alaykum,' Ajmal greeted her as he entered the house. 'Has anna left to open the store? I got a little delayed today. I entered my name at the Tabligh Jamaat Mashora to go to Delhi and then went for the Mashora meeting,' he said walking towards his room.

'When and how long would you be going away for?' Aabida asked, following him.

'A month. We are visiting a lot of places and then finishing at Delhi.'

'Why are you doing all this? Shouldn't you be focusing on the business, on making some money and getting married?' she asked him angrily.

'Allah! What is this strange reaction? I am going to strengthen my faith, my eemaan. We are all seeking good fortune in our next birth. You all believe this life you're living is the only one there is and preoccupying yourself with it. Go away, akka … go find yourself some work to do,' Ajmal said softly but firmly.

Aabida left with a heavy heart. Her face was contorted in confusion and concern for her brother's future. He had completed his BSc with very good marks. When Rasangam had encouraged him to study further, he had refused, saying, 'No, I will take care of the shop with you.' He had studied at Wakf Board College in Madurai. That was where he had been acquainted with the Tabligh Jamaat Mashora. During breaks, he would travel to nearby places for a couple of days with his teachers. A few other students would also join them. That habit had only become stronger since. He was moving away from the conventional desires for higher studies, a good job, a big salary and settling down with a family of his own.

Rasangam worried about him. *I wanted to study further and I didn't have anyone to support my dreams – how is it that his mind is straying into a whole other direction?*

'From now on, you don't need to go to the Tabligh Jamaat or any other such gatherings. Look after the store. Take 25 per cent of the store's profits. Save up, build a house, get married,' he tried telling Ajmal. Ajmal simply smiled in response and waited for the moment to pass. Wishing to hold on to his brother and not let him slip away, Rasangam said, 'I also follow the Eemaan, I pray, I do ilmu, but I also do business – you need money to live well. Why are you so aloof from this world?'

Ajmal sat in silence, fully aware of why his brother was so deeply concerned about him, yet he chose to offer no reply.

29

AJMAL WISHED TO LEAVE THIS PLACE WHERE HE DID not belong and go live somewhere else. This house, where he could sense his sister-in-law's contempt for him, gave him plenty to develop an apathy towards the world. Although he had the choice of going back to his village and take care of the farms and groves there, he had forged a real connection with the nearby mosque, the amir, the people of Tabligh Jamaat; his village held no charm for him. He stayed on here simply because he did not want to go back there.

He had originally come only out of a sense of duty towards his annan, to help out with the store while he was away on Haj, to earn some goodwill. It was Aabida who was perpetually peeved by his appearances and everything he did. If he tried to advise her with a *hadees*, she did not care for it. 'Stop it now. I pray and read the Qur'an myself every day. I don't need you to teach me any hadees,' she would tell him off sternly.

With a medley of thoughts running through his head now, he had a bath and then sat down to eat. Aabida made him some dosai. The silence that filled the space between the two siblings was new, Banu noticed. Aabida's mind was elsewhere. *If he's so devoid of desire, how will we get any girl in the area to marry him?* she worried. *They would be irked by the very sight of him.* She looked again at Ajmal's beautiful face hidden behind his large beard. *What girl living in this day and age would agree to marrying him?*

Rasangam spent several hours reviewing and checking the store accounts. *Ajmal has entered all transactions for all forty days accurately. It didn't appear as if he has kept any money aside for himself. He seems honest and meticulous to a fault. Nothing seems to incite any pride or joy in him, either.* Rasangam sat in quiet contemplation for some time.

Amma and Sachaani had called him the day before. They said Fathima's husband had returned. The man who left right after their daughter was born had returned right after she was married off. Why he had returned, they didn't know. Fathima refused to let him into the house. He was, apparently, staying in the mosque. 'If you could come over, we can discuss what to do now,' Sachaani had said.

He asked Aabida to join him. 'Come, let's go and see him.'

'No, it's okay, you go,' she declined. It was true that there was no need for her to go with him or to meet Fathima's husband, so he quietly acquiesced.

Ajmal wouldn't hold any anger towards his estranged brother-in-law. 'It is all Allah's will,' he would say to solve all problems. Rasangam decided it would make his job easier to take him along on his visit home.

As they set off, Ajmal recited the dua for travel. Rasangam had asked him to drive the car. Somehow, he did not feel like driving today. Moreover, he noticed that Ajmal was a patient driver. He had to look out for Hanifa among the pedestrians on their way as well – it had become a habit. He sat in the front seat, watching his younger brother drive. Baith was playing on the cassette player. 'Have you eaten?' Rasangam asked.

'Yes,' came a short response.

Rasangam began scanning the pedestrians on the street. 'It's September already and it's still so hot. It is supposed to be rainy season, isn't it?' he said.

'It's all different now. There isn't nearly enough *ibaadat* being done in the world. Saithaans have burgeoned and Judgement Day draws near,' Ajmal replied.

Rasangam nodded in seeming agreement. 'For years now, wherever I go, I always scan the streets to see if I can spot any people who seem lost or unstable. So many times I would stop the car to check if one of those people was Hanifa before driving on. Not a day goes by when I don't pray to Allah to see him standing before me.'

'Only if Allah wills it, it'll happen. You are a Haji now. You should entrust all burdens into His care and only keep dua on your lips. Looking out at the streets, searching for him are actions more befitting of someone who has forgotten Him.'

'That's not true, pa. Here we are living in luxury, while he is out there, wandering without food or water. I don't know – I can't eat even one meal in peace.'

Ajmal sensed his brother was overwhelmed and kept quiet. He had always been that way. A little more and he would start crying. Amma would often chide him lovingly, 'Look at you, shedding tears all the time like a woman.'

The sun was directly against them, and blinding. The Baith music continued playing in their silence. Rasangam recalled how, until a few days ago, he used to have songs from movie cassette tapes playing when he travelled by car. *I can't do that anymore, music is* haraam.

'There were a lot of movie cassette tapes here, where did you put them all?' he asked Ajmal.

'You weren't going to listen to them anymore since they are haraam. So, I put them all into a cardboard box and gave it to Aabida. It was sitting in the car trunk for some time. Anni said she wanted to listen to them and took the box away just two days ago.'

Rasangam nodded in approval. 'I bought you a dozen caps, a *musalla* and *tasbih* beads. They are with Aabida.'

Ajmal nodded in acknowledgement.

'I feel like you're not comfortable in this house,' Rasangam said in a very calm and gentle voice. Since he raised the question after much hesitation, he didn't say anything more. *What would thambi's answer be? Will he even give me an answer or would he slip away* – a big burden weighed heavy on his heart.

'Why does no one understand that we're not meant to take anything that we own in this life along with us to our next. Not even people who have faith in Allah – why don't *they* know this?' Ajmal said and flashed his pearly whites at his brother. He had no complaints against anyone; he held no anger, no bitterness.

They were approaching their village.

'There is no need for you to distance yourself from worldly pleasures at your age. Live age-appropriately.' Rasangam let the words out of his mouth despite his hesitance and apprehension, then realized that his younger brother may think of him as being petty and ignoble. He geared up to challenge him.

'We are all just seeking enough good to fill our own graves with, that's all,' Ajmal said, laughing.

Rasangam changed the subject, 'Now you be the one to convince Fathima.'

'I'll talk to her, don't worry,' Ajmal replied confidently.

As soon as they heard the car pulling in, Sainambu and Mahamooda went to the doorway of their house to receive them. Rasangam noticed how the headscarves they had hurriedly pulled over their heads covered more of their faces than usual. He got out of the car and wished them salaam.

'Alaykum salaam,' Sainambu said hugging her son heartily, and kissed him on his forehead.

Fathima's nose pin sparkled on her long nose, locks of curly hair fell on either side of her hair parting. Her face shone brightly but surpassing everything was the fear hidden in her eyes. She was sitting on the threshold of the door to the courtyard with her head hanging down. The four of them surrounded her, each in one direction. She spoke with conviction and clarity, 'Why has that man come back now after so many years? He should not be allowed to enter this house.'

'*Astaghfirullah*! How can you address your husband disrespectfully? That's just wrong, akka,' Ajmal chided her in a tone that was neither soft nor harsh.

'That man was fine. It was she who pushed him around, saying things like he wasn't earning enough, asking if he was even really a man – this witch! The man ran away because he was unable to bear her torture. Did he ever drink like the other men do or go to a prostitute?' Sachaani blew her nose.

'If not for you, how would I or my child have survived? Who would have given my daughter away on her wedding, thambi? You tell me,' her voice rose and ended in a question. She was not being unreasonable.

'Whatever has to happen will happen when it is meant to. When Allah plans, he executes. If you have

out. Without him, it had lost its identity. The posters of film actors Rajni and Kamal that he had pasted on the walls had long been taken down. It didn't smell like him anymore either. It had been too long since everyone had forgotten about his existence and carried on with their lives. He suspected that, more than losing any hopes of his return, they perhaps did not want him to return anymore. Other than Sachaani, hadn't he just been a burden on the others? Like Fathima's husband, Sikandhar, here …

He thought of Rasiya. It would be nice if he could see her. If seven years pass without Hanifa resurfacing, she would be able to remarry. However, he didn't know what her thoughts on the matter were. Fearing that seeing her may kindle his feelings again, he abandoned those thoughts. As he took leave, he placed a wad of cash in his sachaani's hands. He reassured them that he would look after Sikandhar's expenses as well without saying a word.

30

AABIDA LET OUT A SIGH THINKING ABOUT HOW MOST of the village had started avoiding Ajmal and making fun of him.

'That guy, the one who starts quoting hadees,' the young girls in the neighbourhood said referring to him, and laughed within earshot of her, although she pretended not to hear them. These days, Ajmal was spending forty or ninety days going to Tabligh Jamaat conferences.

Whenever he was in town and ran into anyone, he would narrate a hadees to them. The importance of praying, strengthening one's faith, how to prepare for one's next life – these were the only thoughts that consumed him.

'You do your own prayers, why are you pestering everyone else and torturing them? You know they don't value that. When you went to the house across from ours to meet Ayisa's husband Rasaaq, he was there but he told Ayisa to lie that he was not. Do you enjoy this humiliation?' Aabida would say to her younger brother.

'If that is so then so be it. They believe falsely that this life is permanent. Helping them understand otherwise is my moral duty. Is it enough for me to go to heaven alone? I should help others get there too, shouldn't I?' Aabida would quietly observe the deep concern in his eyes.

It had been two months since he had last travelled to places like Mumbai, Hyderabad and Delhi. *It is impossible to find him a bride. Maybe a girl from a less fortunate asarathu family from a neighbouring village would do*, she thought. *He is getting older. We'll refuse dowry and instead, give* mahar *to the bride's family and get them married.*

Ajmal packed away the television set in their living room. 'Annan is now a haji. We cannot have this *saithaan* playing in this house anymore.'

Aabida argued, 'Let it be where it is for us women so at least we can watch something when we want to.'

'No need. Annan will feel uncomfortable.'

Once again, Aabida was left tongue-tied. *When Ajmal goes out of town, we can watch TV*, she decided.

It was hot as an inferno outside. She felt dizzy. The tape recorder and cassette tapes in her room were covered with dust. She wondered how Rasangam was managing without listening to his favourite songs. Banu had said to her, 'Going forward, whenever a new movie is released, we need to call Raman for the cassette tape. He will get it for us.'

Aabida chuckled thinking about the differences between Rasangam and Ajmal. Ever since he had returned from Haj, Rasangam had been very particular that no film music reached his ears. 'It is better to detach from this duniya's pleasures. Please keep me away from all things haraam, ya rabbu!' He would often mumble to himself, 'Ya Allah, strengthen my faith.'

As the villagers talked more and more about how he, the haji, had given up worldly desires at such a young age and now lived in austerity, he confined himself within even more boundaries in his mind. That phase lasted only a short while.

These days, he realized his rigour had waned a little. Even while he was home, Aabida would play songs in her room. She knew which ones he liked. Occasionally, she would turn up the volume before continuing with her chores. Rasangam would appear to be indifferent to the sound and focused on eating or whatever work he was engaged in. Banu would often wonder if he was really detached or if it was merely an act.

When Ajmal was around, however, things were quite different. The whole house fell into a hush. No music was allowed.

'Aabida, come here, I want to talk to you,' Rasangam was standing at the door to Aabida's room.

Maimoona had brought in yesterday's washing which had been hung out to dry on the terrace. Aabida was folding them when she replied, 'I will be right there.' She rose from her cot and came out of her room.

'Where is Banu? Call her,' he said.

She understood that he wanted to talk about something important. She pulled her scarf over her head and with her curiosity growing, walked over to the adjacent room where Banu was. 'Banu, come here for a bit. Rasangam is calling us,' she said to her.

Banu was arranging clothes in her wardrobe. 'What, madhani, is he asking for me?' she asked, hurrying out. She saw her husband sitting in the middle of the hall and asked him, 'My dear, did you need anything? Shall I bring you some tea?'

'I don't need anything. The two of you just come here and sit down,' he said, pointing to the seat across from him.

Aabida and Banu looked at each other. Just as Aabida was sitting down on the sofa, she stopped and said 'I will be back' before rushing into her room to turn off the tape recorder that was playing. She returned and took a seat across from Rasangam, next to Banu.

'It's all good news. We have been approached by a family in Lalpettai who want to marry their daughter to Ajmal. Before I said yes to them, I wanted to check with you and him.'

Aabida looked surprised. *What sort of miracle is this?* her face seemed to say.

'You know how he attends the Tabligh? That girl's

attha also travels with him, I suppose. He is the amir of his village. His name is Ibrahim. He has spent time with Ajmal on their trips and really likes his good habits. Our brother is good-looking, too. So, he decided to reach out to our amir to get my contact information and called me. He is a big man. He owns a supermarket. Because our brother is a good fit for their only daughter, he wants to take him to live with them after the nikkah. He said it would be good to have his support in running the business. I know him too. He is a good man. They are a good family; very wealthy too. I told him I'll have to check with Ajmal. I am not entirely sure if he would agree to relocate to live with them ...' Rasangam trailed off as he drowned in deep thought.

Aabida and Banu were shocked. *What kind of a twist in the story is this?!* They looked at each other and laughed. Aabida adjusted her headscarf and said, 'Ya Allah!' Here I have been worried all year over who would want to give their daughter away to be his wife and look how luck has come seeking him!'

'Hmmm ... but your brother has to agree to move in with them,' Banu griped.

There was no one on the street who did not try to avoid crossing paths with him. Aabida rejoiced in Allah's mercy for blessing him with a good life for the very reason that made the others grumble 'That madman, the minute he sees us, he starts telling us hadees' loudly enough for her to hear. At the same time, she had her reservations about whether he might decline the offer. 'Please, get him to agree to it somehow. I suspect he will start off on some dry *qisa* for a reason to refuse,' her voice sounded troubled.

'We will tell him about it, but if he declines, what can we do? Perform dua. I am expecting the trustee and muttawalli to come home any minute now and discuss the plan for the inauguration of the new mosque. Get some tea or coffee ready. Although maybe buttermilk would be a good option in this sweltering heat.'

The important people in the village are coming all the way to our home to meet Rasangam. He has now become the most important among them. Aabida nearly choked with satisfaction.

'Okay,' the two women said as they got up to return inside the house.

'Please come,' Rasangam invited the visitors in.

'Hajiar, with your help, we have been able to build a new mosque for our village. Thanks to Allah,' said Ismail, the trustee. He greeted him with musafaha and sat down.

'The naataamai sent us here for *mashora*, so we confer with you: Who all we shall invite? How many meals shall we prepare? Please tell us, hajiar,' the muttawalli of the mosque asked, panting from walking in the heat. Because of his rotund physique, it had taken him some effort to haul himself all the way to their house.

'Yes, we will discuss all that. Please, take a minute

to rest first,' Rasangam increased the speed of the fan and urged them to relax. 'What would you like to drink? Something hot or can I offer you some buttermilk?'

'Buttermilk will do, hajiar,' replied Ismail.

'Banu, please bring us some buttermilk, ma,' he said, turning towards the kitchen. 'I have requested the MP of this constituency to be our guest for the inauguration. We will need to set up a stage outside so he can make a short speech. We should make our guests feel honoured. They might feel bad if we don't have a stage. Then, for food, we should serve biryani. As is customary, you will invite the naataamais, muttawalli jamaats and any other important people from the neighbouring villages, will you not? We shall do the same. I will take care of the expenses. Let's not count how many are fed that day. Let there be an abundant supply of food throughout the day. Let anyone who comes partake,' he said. He saw Banu standing at the kitchen door with buttermilk and apples in her hand. He got up to retrieve them from her and serve to his guests. 'Please eat,' he said.

The two men were still struggling to believe their ears. 'Hajiar, you have a very large heart. May Allah grant you *rehmat*,' the muttawalli finally said.

'We came here worried that we would need to go around the village gathering donations to organize the event, but you have lifted that burden off our shoulders. *Jazakallah Alhamdulillah*, Allah is almighty!' Ismail said sincerely as he clasped both of the haji's hands in his own.

'Please eat. Allah has bestowed this abundance upon me. Why thank me?' he said, and continued.

'Please wait a minute. I'll just call the MP's office and confirm the date with them.' He picked up the phone, dialed the number and began to talk to them. From what they could gather from his side of the conversation in English, he was inviting him to Delhi. After he hung up the phone, he said to them, 'His PA has confirmed.'

'Okay, Hajiar, we will take your leave now, please pray all goes well,' Ismail said, getting up to leave.

Since the muttawalli's house was on the street right next to theirs, he told Ismail, 'I'm not coming along with you. I'll go home from here. We will meet at the mosque for asar.'

'I will also take your leave now, hajiar,' he said to Rasangam and got ready to leave.

Aabida watched everything from the window in her room. Listening to them address Rasangam as 'Hajiar' once in every sentence made her ecstatic. She knew just how much her brother had yearned for this respect, this status. Today, that prestige, image and all else he had long desired have finally found their way to him. Tears flowed from her eyes unbeknownst to her. *My own brother* ... she whispered to herself.

Banu rushed out of the kitchen. Her face was stern. Anxious that the two might return, she quickly latched the front door. She stood before her husband, who was seated on the sofa. 'Why have you offered to give them so much money? The whole village contributes to host these public events. What has come over you?!' Her words sputtered like mustard seeds on a hot frying pan.

Rasangam looked up at her patiently. He knew her anger was reasonable. He gently held her arm and motioned her to sit next to him. With a soft smile, he said, 'Isn't all this wealth Allah's gift to us? He will always bless us with good fortune. This money I am spending is based on the calculations I have already made of what percentage of the household's income should go to *jagaat* and how much jagaat we should pay on your jewellery. He continues to give. He has put us in this position where we can afford to give to others. Why make a big deal of it? By getting angry or talking too much about it, we will lose out on the benefits of our goodwill. But you know that already, don't you? "Adam's son, spend on charity and I will spend on you," don't forget that's what Rasul said.'

His calm voice alleviated her anger a little. She lit up. *I must have done something right to have a husband like him*, she contemplated for a second, *a person who always embodies love, never raises his voice, has enough self-control to never yell at anyone, even when he is angry or provoked. In all these years, has he ever left me wanting for anything?* Banu sat pondering quietly. She concluded that she had nothing more to say. She hesitated, wondering for a moment if she had said something wrong to the man who took such good care of her.

Rasangam got up and walked to his room. Aabida came out of her room slowly and wrapped her arms around Banu's shoulders in support.

The whole village was in a celebratory mood. The streets were lined with tubelights and loudspeakers that sounded all day. The smell of biryani was in the air. The men ate to their heart's content and took bucketfuls home for their wives and children. In the evening, the elaborate *pandal* and stage set up close to the mosque and the lively gathering brimming with people was a sight unlike any other. Women sat on their pyols, looking out onto the streets and listening to speeches by important people and the hazrats delivering hadees.

Seated on the stage, were the MP and the MLA alongside the jamaat leaders from neighbouring villages and other religious leaders. Rasangam, too, was seated amidst them. His mind was overflowing with elation at his accomplishment. It was the satisfaction of having carved a place for himself where people had been dismissing him as a nobody. That satisfaction did not feed into any pride or ego; it simply made him feel whole. That by itself was enough. He was no longer seeking anything from God. Anything more could only be termed as greed. He had lost nothing from doing all this. All thanks to Allah. He was sufficient. 'And We wanted to confer favour upon those who were oppressed in the land and make them leaders and make them inheritors,' the Qur'an says, he recalled.

Ibrahim Rawthar from Lalpettai was also present. After Ajmal had consented to the match, Rasangam had sent him an invitation too. Rasangam watched them sitting next to each other in the crowd, listening to the hadees emanating from the stage made and it made him happy.

'He is a sociable and well-mannered person,' Aabida had said that morning when Ibrahim had visited their home.

'A perfect match,' Banu had said and chuckled.

He caught himself thinking about all this while sitting on that stage. He could hardly contain the happiness and peace flowing through his being from within the depths of his heart.

31

THE SECOND YEAR OF COLLEGE HAD COMMENCED. It was five in the evening. The heat had still not let up. It was time for asr. Imran checked his watch for the time.

'Hey silly, stop looking at your watch. Worrying about ibaadat all the time!' Niloufer said, smacking the back of his head gently.

'Go away,' he feigned irritation and smoothed down his hair.

'Why aren't you talking to Anitha at all? You know she cares about you even more than she cares about herself.' This time, Niloufer sounded a little angry.

'So what?' Imran said indifferently.

Dhanasekar figured out easily that he was only pretending to be unaffected. 'Good you asked, Niloufer,' he said, encouraging her.

Imran paused for a second, calmed himself down and looked at the two of them squarely. A breeze blew Niloufer's scarf off her head. With her long fingers, she tried in vain to hold her windblown hair in place. Dhanasekar stood watching, gauging the flow of students exiting the building.

'She is a very nice girl, da. What is your problem? Why you're ignoring a girl to this extent? It's really terrible,' anger flashed across Dhanasekar's face as he spoke and vanished just as quickly. 'Can't believe someone actually likes you with your beard and your personality,' his voice betrayed a little jealousy.

'Why, what's wrong with him? He is the class topper,' Niloufer sprang to Imran's defence.

'Keep your mouth shut, Dhana!' Dhanasekar quietened down seeing Imran flaring up. Niloufer stood there bewildered, not knowing what to say next. A heavy silence weighed down on them.

Imran left them and rushed to the mosque. His father's face flashed before his eyes. 'You are going to Chennai to study, so study well. I never got the opportunity. You finish your studies and you can stay on to work there, if that's what you want to do. Or even go abroad. But wherever you go, keep your faith strong. Be wary of saithaan's temptations,' he recalled his words and his voice overflowing with love as he had prepared to leave home.

'Allah, please protect me,' he began olu.

The next morning, he received a message from Anitha on his mobile. 'Because of me, you behaved badly with Dhanasekar, so I have apologized to him. From now on I will not try to talk to you.'

He felt at ease after reading the message. Without the slightest doubt about whether or not he should reply to her, he decided not to. He felt awkward facing Niloufer when she greeted him with a 'hi', standing outside his class.

'Sorry … where is Dhana?' he asked.

'He's inside, go talk to him. Allah! How do you get so angry?' she expressed her surprise as they entered the classroom together. Very few students were in there, sitting scattered around the room. Not knowing how to face his friend or what to say to him, Imran just sat down next to Dhana. Niloufer went and stood by her seat. Pretending not to notice Imran, Dhana kept his head down, flipping through the pages of the book on his desk.

Imran pressed his right hand in his. 'Sorry, da,' he whispered to him in a low voice inaudible to the others in the room.

Dhana seemed willing to accept his apology. Standing a short distance away from them, Niloufer turned her head slightly to look at them and smiled.

Imran had been fasting since the onset of Ramadan. It was the fifteenth day today and he was a little tired. Even though he faced no trouble finding sahar food at the hostel, his stomach didn't really agree with eating in the middle of the night. He received a phone call from his attha. He reminded him that once he came home after college tomorrow, he would have to make a trip to Madurai to buy Conch Brand lungis, white jibbas, towels, saris and a long list of other things from Madurai for the mosques in the village, the imams, ulamas and others. He thought of his mother. Surely, while attha was talking to him over the phone, his mother would have been standing beside him and grumbling.

'Imran, will *you* at least say something to him? All the money this man earns he has been giving away to all and sundry. If they plan to build a mosque anywhere in the area, they come to him first to collect funds. How is this alright, thambi?' she would ask him in extreme frustration.

Once, during the month of Ramadan, Attha had told her, 'Banu, bring all the jewellery you own. Ask Aabida too. I want all the jewellery in the house.' Sitting on the sofa, he cleared all the papers and books from the big table in front of him to make space for the jewellery. He instructed Imran, 'Take these away and put them elsewhere. Come back with a calculator and sit next to me.'

He never made Imran to do any chores before, but during the month of Ramadan, he would have him do a few odd ones such as this. This wasn't really a chore either. He knew it was his father's way of initiating him into his systems.

'What is all this? This early in the morning? Can we do this a little later? I just woke up after *sahar*.' Without any noticeable frustration or complaint, Amma's voice seemed as if she was imploring to be shown a little consideration since she was fasting.

'I only have a bit of time now. Hurry,' Attha said, rushing her.

With difficulty, amma carried a wooden box and placed it on the table, saying, 'Please wait, let me lock the door in case someone decides to just walk in unannounced.' Scurrying over to the door, she latched it shut. 'First, finish taking stock of this. Then bring Aabida's. Don't mix the two.'

'That makes sense,' Rasangam acceded to Banu's suggestion. Imran sat across from him, looking straight at him. He was wearing a knit cap on his head, a white kaili and a full-sleeved shirt. He appeared to always remain wrinkle-free, even while he slept. His long nose and the mark on his forehead were evidence of his ibaadat to anyone who lay eyes on him.

Attha carefully took every piece of jewellery, weighed it on a weighing scale and read out the weight in grams for Imran to note down. He started adding all the numbers together on his calculator. He teased his mother, 'Why, amma, you have so much jewellery! It is All for my wife, isn't it? It just keeps coming!'

'Of course, who else is it for? Take them and live well, everything here is for your wife. I will give them all to her right at the very outset, as mahar.'

Attha wasn't paying attention to their conversation. Preoccupied, he said, 'That *kaasu maalai*, the 40 sovereign one – it's missing, where is it?'

Amma's face went pale. 'Oh yes, I forgot about it. It's in another box. Even if I forget, you certainly won't!'

'How could I forget? When I returned from Haj, you were so upset that I hadn't bought you any jewellery from Mecca that you made me take you to Madurai just to buy one necklace of 40 sovereigns. How can I ever forget that?' he said and turned to Imran. 'Imran, add 40 sovereigns more.'

Amma said, 'And what did you say to me when you bought it for me? I remember that, too,' with a faint hint of sadness.

'What did you tell her?' Imran asked enthusiastically.

'"When my time comes, you hold onto this for your expenses. Don't rely on anyone for support," that's what he said,' Banu's voice trembled.

What his mother said did not sit well with his father and his face displayed his annoyance. 'Why are you talking about all that? I must've said that in the moment, keep quiet now. Stroking his beard, he added, 'Why are you trying to hide that necklace? The jagaat needs to be calculated based on whatever amount of jewellery we possess to be donated during the month of Ramadan, don't you know that? Do you never remind yourself what the Rasul said?' he added. 'One bedsheet is more than enough for a person. If we possess even a bedsheet more than we need, that belongs to saithaan, does it not?'

Imran had discerned the sorrow in his attha's voice. He understood that he had felt betrayed by his wife's actions.

'Shall we head to the mosque?' Mustafa's voice jolted

Imran back to the present and he hurried out of his classroom. There was still time. 'Allahu,' he muttered as he straightened out his clothes and put on his cap. He started walking to the mosque. He felt his body relax.

As he was settling down to pray to conclude his fast, someone called him on his phone. He continued with his prayers, paying no heed to the call. *It is a mistake not leaving the phone in the room. Getting distracted this way is not good*, he thought and pulled himself together.

It was dark when he stepped out. He didn't feel like eating. He had eaten the customary kanji, vadai and fruits right after he had broken his fast. He decided he would come back when it was time for the taraweeh prayer and made his way to his hostel. Suddenly remembering the call from earlier, he pulled out his phone from his bag.

It was Niloufer. If she had tried to call him right as fasting time was coming to an end, then it must have been something important. He called her, growing a little anxious. He greeted her with a salaam and asked, 'Why had you called at that time?'

'It was nothing ... Anitha had fainted. I called you in panic. She's okay now.'

'Why did she faint? And why did you call me for that?'

'Because she is fasting too, that's why.' Her tone carried a sharp edge. 'You're right, reaching out to you was a mistake. Just let it go.'

Not knowing what to say, Imran stayed silent for a little while. 'But who asked her to fast ... that's so childish. All this has nothing to do with me. Please ...' he said and hung up before he entered his room.

Dhanasekar and Ijaaz were studying there. 'Are you done with your fast? Ijaaz returned a while ago – why are you late?'

Imran understood why Dhanasekar had been expecting him earlier. He went and lay down quietly on his bed. *What is this madness? She chose to recite the Kalima and convert to Islam; she chose to pray five times, won't wear a bindi, and now she is fasting*, he muttered inwardly and ground his teeth. *This love is doomed to fail even in her dreams. Has she really lost her senses completely that she can't see it?* Every time he wanted to see Anitha, his attha's face came to mind. He wasn't prepared to think about anything else either.

'Can you not explain my situation to that girl and how different it is from her situation?' he remembered discussing with Niloufer once. He wasn't particularly interested in Anitha and it had never been in his nature to spend too much time daydreaming about something that was never going to happen.

When the entire family was so committed to ibaadat, to fall in love with a Malayali Hindu girl and then try to marry her was a complete waste of everyone's time, he had no doubts about that.

'Her religion and her family are by no means below yours, you know,' Dhanasekar had once told him rather strongly. Imran had noticed Dhana's short, bulky body tremble with anger. His flat face struggled to hide his ire.

'So be it. Now you may as well go and tell her yourself not to waste her time.' Imran too had been quite firm that day.

'Did Niloufer call you?' Dhanasekar asked. Imran turned to face the other way and gave no answer.

The deafening silence and oppressive heat in the room worsened the tension in his mind. He noticed how the branches of the neem tree outside the window next to his cot were completely still. The tree that looked like a photograph, the sky stretching above it and dotted with stars unsettled him. Unable to distinguish his loneliness from emptiness, he felt his mind and body grow weary. He doubted if he would be able to sleep. At some point, he drifted off to sleep.

Because it was a Sunday, Imran woke up late. He had to leave that night to go home. He was yet to buy the things his attha had asked him to bring along. He did not need to return to college until after Eid. He packed the clothes he needed and some books in a suitcase. He placed the Qur'an carefully in his desk and locked it. Dhanasekar and Ijaaz had not yet woken up. He stepped out of his room. He had woken up at four this morning to state the *niyyat* and pray without eating anything at sahar.

He stood in front of his college canteen and looked around. The sun's rays beat down on his back. The canteen was largely empty except for a couple of boys drinking tea. The neem tree shade and the soft breeze felt comforting. Under the tree, he laid out his handkerchief around the base of the tree and sat atop it carefully without getting his clothes dirty. 'Imran,' he heard someone call out to him. He turned around to see who it was. Anitha was approaching him.

'What is it?' he asked, trying to get up.

She stopped him. 'Wait, let me also sit down,' she said freely, and sat down on a small rock lying on the ground opposite him, facing him head-on. She had a lanky body and fair skin, on her round face, her eyes appeared sunken. The thick locks of her hair that spilled over her face rolling down made her look beautiful, although she seemed tired.

He remembered she was fasting. Yet, he chose to feign ignorance. It was only today that he was taking a good look at her. For the first time, his mind registered her face.

She looked straight at him and asked, 'Why are you leaving for home already?'

'The school is closed, so why not?'

'Niloufer is leaving only tomorrow. That's why I ask.'

'Maybe she's bored of her hometown and wants to spend an extra day here with her friends.'

She realized this was not what she had come to talk to

him about. *Why am I talking about something completely unrelated like a fool?* She remained silent for a few minutes. She seemed to be staring at something faraway. For some reason, he felt uncomfortable. A couple of neem berries rustled as they fell from the tree. She ran her fingers through her hair, tousled by the breeze. The way her blue salwar and dupatta moved in the breeze stirred something within him. He watched her closely. She wasn't wearing a bindi. She did not have so much as an ounce of extra fat on her body. *Does she eat at all?* he wondered. *If she decides to fast in this condition, she is bound to faint.*

'Why are you making things harder for you? I never said I love you. Then why do you choose to recite Kalima, become Muslim and offer prayers like a Muslim? This is all nonsense,' he wanted to word his disapproval more strongly, but he failed.

'I like you. I will do anything for you. Understand that!' Her childlike voice touched his heart.

What sort of foolishness is this? Shouldn't she be a little more mature about this, he wondered, feeling sorry for her. He did not know what else to say to her. How was he supposed to make a girl so pure and innocent understand all this? He started feeling concerned about her. A girl who was so good at her studies was now imagining things and deceiving herself.

'Okay, you leave now, we will talk later.' He wanted her to go away. He hoped she would discern his faith in your religion, if you believe in the strength of your prayers, do sabur.' Rasangam's words prevented Fathima from saying anything more. After having spent his entire youth away from home, her estranged husband had returned now as a sick man. Just being told that it was her duty to dedicate the rest of her life to taking care of him irritated her. She could not get herself to agree to accepting a man who had chosen not to live with her through the ups and downs of life and whom she had finally managed to almost erase from her memory. But she had neither the courage nor the freedom to refuse.

Ajmal went to the mosque and brought home the man who appeared much older than his years. Rasangam embraced him, did musafaha, and gave him a proper welcome. Instead of giving him new kailis and jibbas in his hands, he placed them in his room. Time had transformed the handsome, energetic man he had seen in his youth and on the day of his wedding with Fathima into a beggar standing before him now; that change was greatly agonizing to see. He looked pathetic as he stood there in front of them, haggard and hunched over. His unkempt beard and weather-beaten, frail body brought tears of pity to their eyes.

Rasangam prayed to God from the bottom of his heart that no matter what the circumstance, no man should ever be forced to stand before their family in as sorry a state, begging to be forgiven and accepted. He looked around Hanifa's room once and then came undertone. She rose, feeling greatly disappointed. Her face had flushed with shame. He was still looking at her wondering what he could do to help her see sense as she turned around and walked away from him.

'You think you are too smart!' he remembered Niloufer yelling at him once. He believed that his ability to be pragmatic was his strength. His attha had often told him that getting too caught up in things that would never see the light of day was simply a waste of his time. Those words had made a very big impact on him.

Imran never ignored the lessons his father shared with him based on his life experience. Who could deny that the path his father had walked and the destination he had reached were owed to those very lessons? He got up to leave. Standing up, he looked in the direction she had gone. For the first time, her body lithe like a slender minaret made his heart flutter. It boosted his ego that a girl loved him so much, she was ready to do anything for him.

'Allahu, whatever You deem, I shall accept. I will walk the path you show me. *Auzu billahi minash saithaan nirajeem*,' he said as he walked to his hostel room.

32

A PHONE CALL HAD BROUGHT THE NEWS THAT Fathima's husband was not doing well. It had been from Shameema.

Rasangam did not visit home often enough. He still hadn't been able to forget about Hanifa. Whenever he travelled, his eyes still searched for him on the streets. Seven years after his disappearance, Rasangam had sent money to Rasiya and encouraged her to remarry. Amma had gone to give her the money, but she had refused it.

'Such arrogance and obstinacy – that crazy bitch!' He remembered how frustrated his mother had sounded. He would usually go to the village every year just to give jagaat to relatives and friends. *If I go tomorrow, I can also visit Fathima's husband*, he thought.

'Attha, shall we leave? There are only ten more minutes until the fasting ends. We will reach before the modinar's call to prayer,' Imran's voice brought Rasangam back to the present. He straightened up and looked at his son. It made his heart swell with pride to see his son so immersed in ibaadat. He was tall with a longish face red with pimples. His bright face and beautiful appearance made his father mutter '*Masha'Allah*', before saying, 'okay, let's leave,' and getting up to go to the mosque with his son.

'Let's go by bike. Come, you can sit behind me,' Imran pulled out his bike. Rasangam sat pillion.

The mosque was teeming with people. More than people seated in queues to break their fast were hawkers visiting from other places and students flocking to them. The air was buzzing with the excitement of festivities. Imran relished the celebratory spirit, the fragrance of the fasting kanji, and other delicious foods evoked. As he reflected that, no matter where he went, returning to his village for the month of Ramadan always filled him with a sense of deep satisfaction, Anitha suddenly came to his mind. *She would have gone to her hometown, too. Will she be thinking about me there as well?* That thought kindled an instant happiness within him. He should call her and check if she was still fasting when he got back home. He realized he had never been this way all these days. *Why think about any of this when the focus should be on fasting and the breaking of fasts?* He muttered 'Astaghfirullah' to pull himself out of these thoughts.

Imran and Kailasam together loaded the saris, kailis, shirts and other packages into the car trunk. It was a Tavera, so there was plenty of room. Rasangam was satisfied. 'Okay, let's go. Start the car,' he said, adding, 'Aabida, come on, ma, get in the car.'

'I'm coming!' she said rushing out and clambered into

the back seat. Her body being rather heavy for her age she panted for breath. 'Usss Allahu,' she exclaimed and spread her legs to sit comfortably. 'Banu has declined to join us because she wants someone to stay at home. That is alright, too. People come looking for jagaat all day. They will feel disappointed to find the house locked,' she said.

'What is Banu going to do there anyway? There's no need for her to come,' Rasangam said, echoing his sister's thoughts. 'Okay, let's leave now. Kailasam, you go to the store. We're leaving now.'

'Okay, master,' Kailasam said and left.

Imran chanted the dua for safe travels and started the car.

'Will Ajmal also come to our hometown today?' asked Aabida.

'Yes, he is coming too. He would be closer. Sarahamma and the children are coming too,' Rasangam replied.

'The children are coming too? That's great! It's been a while since I saw them,' Aabida said joyfully.

Imran also felt cheerful. 'This is the only way we get to see the children, isn't it, attha? Only once or twice a year.'

'Yes, they've got school. They can't visit on a whim, can they? In our days, we went to school if we felt like it and didn't go if we didn't. These days, there is no chance they allow all that,' Rasangam said, smiling, before he turned to scan the streets through his window out of habit. *Will God never make Hanifa appear in front of my eyes?* he wondered wistfully. Both Imran and Aabida knew very well what he was looking out of the window so ardently for. They paused the conversation. This search spanning several years. Aabida started praying, counting the beads in the tasbih in her hand.

They knew Ajmal had already reached home before they did by the noise the children made. Imran stacked all the packages on the pyol of the house. The heat was finally on the decline.

Ajmal greeted his elder brother with musafaha. When he came to Imran, he said, 'Look at you! Don't you look all grown up and good looking, just like a bridegroom!' before greeting his brother's son with musafaha as well. The overwhelming smell of his attar emanating from his shoulders suffocated Imran.

Relatives began to drop in. 'The Hajiar has come, we came to see him and greet him with musaba,' Kasim Lebbay said and Rasangam embraced him and did musafaha. 'How are you, thambi? It has been such a long time since I last saw you,' the flesh on his old face had softened its grip and was shaking in happiness. The kaili he wore up to his ankles had become threadbare. The overwhelming joy in his eyes warmed Rasangam's heart.

'Salaam, machaan,' Sarahamma greeted him from her room in a clear voice.

Aabida went into the room and said, 'Since you are inside the house, you can remove your *purdah* and use the end of your sari to cover your head.'

'Let it be, macchi,' she said with a smile. Her face was bloodless and pale.

Fathima's husband was lying on a cot in his room with his legs outstretched. His asthma made it difficult for him to breathe.

'Salaam, machaan,' Rasangam and Ajmal greeted him and sat down on the chairs by his bed. He held Rasangam's hands in his. His body had become thin as a stick. With his health having deteriorated so drastically, he seemed to have lost all hope of living.

Imran hugged all four of his little sisters – Saheena, Shaanya, Shaakira and Aayisha – who stuck to their mother Sarahamma's side and started playing with them. Aabida felt bad that all four of Ajmal's children were girls. She could not get herself to talk to Ajmal about contraception, nor could she talk to Sarahamma. They were truly made for each other. 'We cannot betray Allah,' was their answer to everything.

Sarahamma had become rather weak; she was pale and skinny. *Only if she removes her purdah, I can see the rest of her. But she will never. That's the sort she is,* Aabida thought, displeased. The girl who appeared ripe as a red apple on the day of her nikkah had now become flat and thin as a cluster bean.

Rasangam too had tried to warn Ajmal. 'Please take care of her, pa. She doesn't have any flesh on her. She is becoming very weak.' Ajmal did not pay heed to any of it.

'Why is this girl wearing purdah even inside the house?' Aabida mumbled under her breath. She felt stifled by the mere sight of her.

Sachaani and Fathima were chatting with Aabida. 'This man disappeared when we could have lived happily together and has come to me at the end of his life to suck whatever life I have left in me. I don't know what will get me to shed a tear when he passes on ...' Fathima said bitterly to Aabida. She then said, 'Come, everyone has arrived. Let's go break our fast,' and brought Aabida out of the room into the courtyard.

Shameema and two other ladies had spread mats all over the front yard and arranged the kanji, sherbet, fruits, vadai, bajji and other dishes in big vessels in a row. They used plates and tumblers to serve everyone. Rasangam and Ajmal came out into the courtyard as well. Coming to their hometown like this to meet all their relatives every year, having *Iftar* together and doing charity before returning home brought them great satisfaction.

The yard was large enough to host a hundred people. Rasangam was elated at the sight of all their relatives and people from the village gathering to feast together. After the guests had broken their fast, they placed a package of clothes that he and his brother had bought, along with an envelope containing money in each person's hand before seeing them off. When they were finally getting ready to go back home, Mahamooda leaned on Rasangam's shoulder and said, 'How did I let Hanifa run away, attha?' and began crying.

'Do sabur … Allah is sufficient. He knows. He will definitely let us see annan one day,' Rasangam reassured Mahamooda and got into his car. Imran noticed how his attha's voice had become feeble.

Just as Rasangam sat in the car, he was reminded of Rasiya. *Why didn't she come today? If I had called, would she have come?* he wondered. He knew she would not have. If he were to meet her, it would not be easy for him to face her. *It is for the best that she did not come*, he concluded and calmed himself down.

'Anne, shall I also leave?' Ajmal asked Rasangam for permission.

'Come to our place for the big feast, attha,' Aabida invited her younger brother over.

'I have to give jagaat; there's just a lot of work to do. We will come another day, akka, *Inshallah.* Bye.'

Rasangam did not insist. The two brothers took each other's leave. Imran did not want to leave his sisters and continued to play. Every time they met, he wanted to listen to their laughter and chatter endlessly. Still, he reluctantly gave them a tight hug and bid them adieu and wished Sarahamma salaam.

When Rasangam said 'start the car, pa', it was already eight. 'We have to reach home by *taraweeh.* Drive like you must to make that happen,' he told his son.

'Why does he have such a long beard? Can't he keep it trimmed like yours?' Aabida complained about her younger brother.

'Shh ... we'll talk later,' Rasangam said, putting a stop to it.

Amma, sachaani and Fathima stood outside, looking sad. Rasangam was choked with sorrow at leaving his mother behind. Even though her children were living in luxury, she was not prepared to live with them. 'My husband built this house. I want to live out my days here,' she was adamant.

Living with sachaani is, in a way, a huge support for her, he pacified himself. Driving through the streets enveloped in darkness, the car left the village.

'Sarahamma has become very thin, hasn't she? If she keeps bearing a child a year, how will her body ever recover?' Aabida said, annoyed.

'One has to move with the times and changing circumstances. The Tabligh fellows don't understand this. They live in their own world worrying only about the next life. Islam is a way of life. He can dress well. Instead, he wears these oversized jibbas ...' Rasangam said and let out a disgruntled sigh.

A message chimed on Imran's phone which was kept between the two front seats. He bent to see who it was from. It was Anitha. Four more messages popped up one after the other, drawing Aabida's attention to his phone. He noticed her bending forward to see who was messaging him. He quickly took the phone in his hand, put it on silent and dropped it into his shirt pocket.

'He doesn't see himself as being extreme. Instead, he keeps finding faults with us all the time and saying that we don't follow eemaan properly,' Rasangam continued to rant about Ajmal. His anxiety made Imran worry. He said, 'Let it go … what he believes to be Islam, he follows. You believe what you believe, he believes in a different way.'

'That is not it. Understanding the Qur'an and living by it is the right way. He has to live with a consideration for reality, doesn't he? That is my concern. See now, this girl's body has withered away. He will not send his daughters to study. The way the world is today, it is important for both men and women to be educated. When the whole world has only hatred towards our society, we too need to become progressive to keep up with the times. Education and getting government jobs are the best option. Instead of that, putting them in burqas and confining them to their homes – how is that fair? He will give his daughters away in marriage when they turn fifteen. How can I not be worried seeing all this happen in front of my eyes?'

'That's right, are we not following Islam?' Aabida echoed Rasangam's concern.

They were both in agreement. Imran drove faster. If they had to reach by the taraweeh prayers, he needed to drive faster. He noticed that Aabida kuppi, who usually complained if he drove fast, sat quietly and smiled softly. It was clear that her mind was wandering elsewhere. Because it was dark outside, his attha was no longer scanning the streets. Instead, he closed his eyes and leaned back in his seat.

Instead of offering the taraweeh prayers, Banu was sitting on the front pyol, waiting for them.

'What are you so afraid of, amma? We went to the village right here,' Imran teased his mother.

'Even when I drive, she panics and wants me to come back before sundown. This time it is her son – won't she panic even more? Believing in Allah and leaving it to His will is not an option for her,' Rasangam laughed.

'Go on and mock me,' Banu grumbled. 'How was everything – the iftaar, was there a good crowd this year? How is kuppi and everyone else?' she asked eagerly.

'Yes, there was a huge crowd. You missed it,' Aabida said, jaded. She didn't think Banu was going to ask about Ajmal. So she went into her room to perform olu without saying anything about him.

'How is Fathima's husband doing?'

'Not well. He is struggling to breathe now, we will do dua for him. Okay, come. Let's pray,' she took her musalla in her hand and gave it a shake.

By the time Imran went into his room upstairs to sleep, it was already twelve. He would have to wake up again by three-thirty for sahar. His eyes were burning. Fatigue had overtaken his body. Driving the car since the afternoon without any rest, going to the village – it had all added up. He pulled out his phone to check the messages.

'Where are you now? How are you?' Anitha's message said. *She has sent it four days after returning home. Maybe she was hesitant to message earlier and waited until today to send it.*

It would be rude not to respond. He sent her a reply: 'Aren't you asleep yet?'

'I'm just going to sleep,' she replied, 'Because I'm home, I can't fast anymore.'

For the first time ever, the two of them spent some time exchanging text messages that night. Only when his mother called him on the phone for sahar meal, he realized he had spent all that time with her. 'Pch,' he reproached himself. His mind had wavered. A fear that he had paid attention today to something he had chosen to ignore all these days grew within him. The anger and solemnity he had been able to display when they had met in person, he was no longer able to keep it up and that puzzled him.

When he woke up in the morning, he felt so light-hearted. He couldn't remember if he had ever felt this way before. He could feel his love for Anitha welling up. He wondered if maybe being apart for a whole week may have had something to do with it. On the days he fasted, he usually felt lethargic in the mornings. But today, he felt as though fresh blood was pumping through his body. The thought of being loved by a girl so deeply gave him a sense of boundless joy – a joy that he never had experienced before.

33

'Imran, come here, attha,' Attha's voice brought Imran back to reality.

'What is it, attha?' he said, entering his room. Rasangam was sitting on his cot and stroking his beard, lost in thought. Imran went closer and stood next to him, quietly waiting for him to speak.

Amma entered the room, her hurried footsteps causing the floor to vibrate. She hesitated slightly when she saw the father and son together. Imran caught her eye and gestured her to go away, and she gently retraced her steps. He noticed his father slowly opening his eyes. They always reflected an inner peace and compassion. Today, Imran observed they seemed even more so than usual. 'Your attha is an *avuliya*, Imran,' Aabida kuppi's words echoed in his mind in that instant.

'Imran, have you taken a bath?' his father asked, drawing his attention.

The sunrays forcing their way into the room through the window, the fragrance of his attha's attar in the air calmed his mind greatly. Aabida kuppi's 'he is an avuliya, your attha' echoed in his ears once again.

'Yes, attha, I have.'

'Come closer, come sit,' he placed his hand on the cot to indicate where Imran should sit. 'Now, during the month of Ramadan, read the Qur'an and what is prescribed as the right way of life in the hadees, okay?'

Imran nodded his head in acknowledgement, but his face betrayed his confusion. *What's the problem, what's he trying to say?* He remained silent. When he was a young boy, his attha had bought him a Tamil edition of the Qur'an. 'Attend the madrasa, they will teach you the Qur'an only in Arabic. You can read it in Tamil so you understand the meaning and find it useful in leading your life,' he had told him. Imran looked at him patiently.

'You have been seeing me do charity during this month of Ramadan, whom I donate to and how I calculate how much to donate. I wish for you to always follow the same. To Him who gave us all this luxury, abundant opportunities, wealth, cars, people's respect, all we have – we must give our thanks all the time. At the same time, don't live like Ajmal. His beliefs are entirely removed from this life. He only talks and thinks about the afterlife,' he heard the resolve in his father's voice. 'He has had four daughters in a row. He refuses to stop to think about them or their future, or about the toll on Sarahamma's health. He doesn't pay attention to his business. Wherever the Tabligh Jamaat goes, he goes,' he continued. Imran understood this part. But he couldn't figure out why his father was saying all this now, out of the blue. He had never spoken to him like this before. So why today?

'What are you thinking about? Don't be scared, I just felt like talking to you, that's all. You have grown past my shoulder, what can I possibly teach you now? You already know all this. Still, isn't it my duty to educate you about *halal*, haraam and how to live life based on my experiences? That's all,' his attha said, letting out a sigh. 'Okay, you go get ready now. A shipment has arrived at the shop from Mumbai. We need to take account of it and put the goods away. Come, let's go.' He called out to his amma, 'Banu?'

'Yes?' she said, entering the room. Imran noticed the utter confusion on his mother's face.

'I will send you a list of ulamas and asarathus from the shop. Get packages of kailis and shirts ready to send to them. Imran will go to the mosques in all the neighbouring villages and hand them out the afternoon, during luhar. Won't you, son?' Rasangam said, neither as a command nor a request.

'I'll go, Attha,' Imran answered politely. Rasangam placed his hands on his shoulders and pressed them gently as he said, 'Okay then, we're leaving.'

Just then, Aabida came in hurriedly. 'That Karuppan, he said his daughter is getting married and has asked for some money. When should I ask him to come back?'

'Tell him to come to the store in the morning.'

The two left the house. 'Imran, I will drive today. You

sit next to me.' Imran reflected on his father's efforts to guide him towards a better future. 'Once you are done with your studies, whether you want to study further or work or come back and take care of the store … whatever it is you might want to do, you are free to choose. Do you understand?' he looked at his son and smiled.

Imran wanted to hug his father tightly. His heart swelled with tenderness.

A whole lot of goods had arrived at the shop. Thahir took stock of all the goods. Unlike the case twenty years ago, there was no longer a demand for bicycle spare parts since people did not use bicycles as much. There was a much higher demand for parts of scooters, bikes and electronic items. *Isn't that what happens as times change? The tape recorder was all the rage earlier; now there are mobiles and televisions*, Rasangam chuckled to himself. *He can take care of this business. But if he doesn't want to, that's okay too. In this day and age, it is far more important to get an education and a decent job*, he ruminated.

After all, based on the Jamaat's suggestion, it was Rasangam who provided annual financial aid to the children who excelled in school in their village. 'Wouldn't you rather contribute to kumaru so the poor families can marry off their daughters?' the trustee had asked him.

'We will, but we will give priority to education first,' Rasangam had replied, silencing the trustee and all the others.

'Attha, should I send Thahir home to pick up the clothes packages?' Imran asked, bringing Rasangam back from his thoughts.

'Yes, yes, send him. It's getting late. You have to go to eight villages in the area.' He opened his cupboard to take out the list. 'Here, look at this. I have written down all the details of jagaat, whom we donate to and how much we have donated every year so far, in this notebook here. Here are all the details of the asarathus and ulamas – their names and addresses. Get a copy of this, return the notebook to me and send the photocopy home so you can tally the number of packages. You can then take the list along with you when you go to drop off the packages. Tell amma to send them over,' he instructed his son.

Imran listened to his father's soft yet firm voice and replied, 'Okay, attha. I'll get a photocopy made.' He took the notebook from him.

'Remember to bring it back to me,' his attha said before returning to review the accounts.

No one was at the Xerox shop. Rasaaq had stepped out, and Imran didn't know when he would return. The heat was harsh even as the sun was still only rising. He flipped through the notebook. Most of it was full of details of the charity work his attha had done during the month of Ramadan. Along with those, he had also scribbled some notes on contributions he had made towards some children's college education. *He likely wrote it all down just so he wouldn't miss making further payments for any of them in the coming years. He had been doing this for so many years now. But why did he suddenly feel the urge to share all this with me this year? Why had he suddenly started advising me?* Imran didn't quite understand, but he also felt like he did, somewhat.

34

'SALAAM ALAYKUM, ANNE! WHEN DID YOU COME?' Rasaaq greeted Imran as he entered the Xerox shop.

'Just now, da. Where did you go, where is attha?' Imran asked.

'He was feeling a little tired from the fasting, so he's gone home to rest. The heat is really tormenting too,' he answered wearily. 'Why, anne, do you need a copy of that? Give it to me,' he said, reaching out for the notebook.

'Yes, here, I just need a xerox of these two pages.' Imran gave him the notebook with the pages open. The shop was a tiny ten by ten room. It was really dusty. Files were piled up in messy stacks all over a table. All the dust from vehicles passing through the street flew right into the shop.

'Here you go, anne. Done,' Rasaaq said, handing the notebook and the copies of the two pages to Imran. 'When does your college reopen, anne?'

'Four days after Eid. What about yours?'

'Mine opens around the same time too.'

'You study in Trichy, right?' Imran asked. 'And how much for the copies?'

'Ada, let it go anne. Hardly two pages, how can I take money from the Hajiar? He is the reason I am able to go to college.' Even though this was news to Imran, he wasn't really surprised.

'Okay, I will see you then,' he said as he got ready to leave.

'Did you walk here in this heat?'

'Yes, our shop is just two shops over, why bring the bike just for this distance?'

'The left hand shall not know what the right hand gives,' he had heard his father say many times. He had discovered only today that his father was the one paying for Rasaaq's education. He had never made any mention of this to him. Today, the information had found its way to him all on its own. He had no idea how many more children his father was helping in this way.

He was reminded of an interaction between God and the angels:

Angels: God, amongst all your creations, what is stronger than a mountain?

God: Iron.

Angels: And what is stronger than iron?

God: Fire.

Angels: What is stronger than fire?

God: Water.

Angels: What is stronger than water?

God: Wind.

Angels: And what is stronger than all of them?

God: A man whose left hand does not know what his right hand gives.

He thought of his father with pride.

As he prepared to set off from the shop, his father reminded him once again: 'Make sure you say to every aalim that your attha said salaam. Request them to do dua for us. Give one package and one envelope to each,' he made an earnest attempt to ensure the significance of the act was impressed upon his son's mind. 'Also, don't remove your cap. Go now and come back soon.'

'Okay, attha,' Imran said and started the car. There were only seven places in all, not eight, and they were all located in the neighbouring villages. He estimated he would be able to wrap up the task in two or three hours.

Just then, he heard the message tone on his mobile. Anitha's name flashed on the screen. She had sent four messages, one after another, and her name was stacked in four rows. He instantly remembered how her messages had caused his phone to chime continuously when he was sitting next to his father the previous night. He figured his attha would surely have noticed her name and that helped lift the fog surrounding his peculiar behaviour that morning.

He suddenly felt as if he had lost something. His body shuddered a little. His heart raced and he began to sweat. He parked the car on the side of the road under a tree, turned up the air conditioning and sat quietly for some time. He could see cows grazing on the foothills. The agave plants absorbing the searing midday heat, the black babul trees and overgrown shrubs, all stood still in absolute silence. In ten more minutes, he would arrive at the first village he was supposed to go to. His mind refused to muster up the courage to pick up his phone and check the messages. After sitting calmly for a few minutes, he started driving again.

Driving back home after completing his task, he felt that the mosques he had visited and all the hazrats and ulamas he had met that day had been content with the charity. 'You are Hajiar's son? Ya Allah,' the way he was greeted and the respect he had been shown had intimidated him. When they talked compassionately about the contributions and help that his father had extended to them for the construction of these mosques, Imran had felt distressed. *So much respect, so much love* ... He staggered at all the work he had done for his community. The love he had for his father transformed into tremendous respect. More than being awestruck, learning about his father's charity and hard work to improve the lives of people around him had left Imran feeling a greater sense of responsibility.

There was not an inkling of doubt now about the message his attha had wanted to convey to him through his words and the tasks he had assigned to him.

Parking the car in the portico, he walked into their

house with the ardent desire to see him right away and hug him tightly. Imran resolved that he would never let his actions cause any harm to his father or his prestige.

It was three in the afternoon. Aabida kuppi was sitting in the middle of the living room. *Attha must be taking a nap in his room.* 'Kuppi, why are you sitting here by yourself? Fasting usually makes you drowsy, are you not going to take a nap?' he asked her.

'No, attha. I had been lying down all this while. It is our turn to provide the fasting kanji today. They will send some over to our house from the mosque. I'm just sitting around, waiting to receive it.' She sighed. Her fatigue was evident from her face. 'Have you been everywhere you were supposed to go, attha? What did they say? Did they say they will do dua?' Even though she asked sincerely, he felt as if she was asking for the sake of making conversation.

'Yes, yes, I met everyone. It was very nice, satisfying,' he replied. 'All those ulamas have so much respect for attha … It gave me goosebumps, kuppi.'

'The struggle your father has had to endure to get here … Allah! Allah is sufficient.' She pressed both her palms against her chest.

'Indeed, kuppi. Allah is sufficient,' he said, sitting next to her and removing his shirt.

'Give that to me, attha, I will get it washed,' she said, holding her hand out.

'I'll put it in the laundry hamper. You stay here.'

Aabida looked at him closely. He was a spitting image of Rasangam. The same nose, forehead, eyes. 'When I look at you, it is exactly as if I was looking at your father in his younger days,' she said.

'He was as thin?'

'Yes, he looked like he was going to snap into two any minute. He was so patient … such a good man, so wise …' she said absentmindedly.

Imran sat on the floor and kept his gaze fixed on her. She had the same tender face as his attha. The fullness of her face had begun sagging because of age. She must have been very beautiful in her heyday, though. Traces of it still lingered in her face. She lived a selfless life and wanted nothing for herself. He had witnessed the strength of the love between his father and his kuppi in many situations. He wished all the time that he had a sister like her too. Occasionally, when amma would just say something thoughtlessly in her excitement, kuppi would handle the situation patiently and tactfully.

'What is it, attha? You are staring at me? Your kuppi wishes she had a daughter of her own,' she said and smiled. When she smiled, it really felt as if a flower was blooming.

'Yes, kuppi. I was thinking about how beautiful you must have been when you were younger. That's all.'

'I sure am getting old,' she said and laughed quietly. 'Okay, you go and get some rest now. I am also going to take a nap.' Imran curled up next to her and rested his head on her lap. The warmth of her body felt comforting. 'What attha, why so suddenly?' she asked, panicking a little.

'Just like that. Just let me lie here for a little while,' he said.

He had so many fond memories of his kuppi. He had grown up lying in her lap and listening to her stories. Whenever amma got angry and scolded him, he would hide in her lap and seek. Her mind was full of thoughts only about Rasangam, Banu and Imran. He had never known her to think about anything else beyond them. Every time he got too close to kuppi, his mother's face would betray some displeasure, enough for him to step away or hesitate.

Anytime he showed kuppi the slightest favour, he saw his mother erupt with anger at kuppi. His heart would be crushed under the weight of the hostility directed towards kuppi. He found her serene face and her extraordinary detachment from everything material eternally fascinating.

'What, attha? Seems like you want to tell me something,' she hugged him warmly. 'You must protect your father's reputation. Don't you ever forget it, darling.' Her soft voice and her words neither sounded instructive nor pleading and caressed him like a gentle breeze. Imran mentally embraced the softness in her voice as tightly as he could.

By the time he finished praying and left for home with attha on the day of Eid, he had had enough. Due to the sudden heavy rains the previous night, the *kutba* prayer could not be offered outside on the street. However, the new mosque stood within such spacious grounds that everyone was able to offer their prayers inside its premises. Everyone was delighted that there was ample space. People who were travelling on business as well as those who were visiting from the Arab nations were very extremely satisfied at being able to pray inside the new mosque. He felt proud when everyone there had hugged attha and greeted him with musafaha to thank him and express their contentment. Attha too had happily exchanged good wishes with them. The scent of new clothes and attar clung to the nostrils. The light drizzle, cool breeze, the musallas spread out across the floor and the cold new marble underneath his feet filled his heart with joy and prompted him to utter 'ya Allah' loudly without even realizing it. He had been so excited, he wanted to embrace his father right there. It took some effort to rein himself in.

Over the last two days, he had felt a sense of relief that Anitha hadn't once crossed his mind. From here on there was no more room for confusion – the answer was clear. Luckily, he hadn't yet told her he loved her too. *We've just casually been exchanging messages. I can't afford to bring any disgrace to attha's name or reputation,* he decided. In that large crowd, his attha, with his white skullcap and a towel from Mecca thrown over his shoulder, had looked just like a Sufi.

Imran entered his hostel room but felt too tired to put his suitcase away in the right place. He had not been able to sleep well in the overnight train. Since it was almost time for fajr, he quickly informed his father of his safe arrival and left to do olu. He heard the call for prayers from the mosque. He observed his face in the bathroom mirror for a few minutes. His beard had grown too much. While he had been at home, there had been no need to trim it or even think about trimming it. He decided to trim it after his prayers.

'Why didn't you send me even one message?' Anitha's voice from the desk next to his in their classroom suddenly made him look up from his book. He looked at her as though he just regained consciousness.

'What deep thought were you lost in? You didn't even notice us come in,' Niloufer winked and laughed.

'It's nothing … just like that,' he smiled sheepishly and kept quiet, trying to dodge Anitha's question by pretending as if he had forgotten all about it. He did this knowing full well that it would hurt her. He decided it would help to portray himself as a bad guy.

'Okay, okay, stop thinking about your village now.

Anitha asked you a question.' It was clear Niloufer had made it her mission not to let him get away so easily.

'I didn't have the time. That's why I didn't respond,' he responded while looking at Niloufer, which Anitha found strange. *What is up with him?* she wondered. She felt that they had grown apart again. Niloufer's face seemed to tell her that she had the answers to quell her confusion. She was pulled out of the moment by the growing sound of chatter in the classroom.

Later, they were sitting in the canteen. 'Are you mad, da?' Niloufer said, rapping his head with her knuckles.

'Pch … stop it,' Imran said, then chanted 'Bismillah' before sipping on the tea that he was holding in his hand.

'Then why did you lead her on by exchanging messages with her all through that night, until dawn?' Her stern round face was red with anger.

'Niloufer, you and I can sit here and talk about this endlessly. But when I'm at home with my family, I can't afford to be thinking about it all. You come from Ramanathapuram – you know how things would go, won't you? Then why are you pestering me this way, tell me?' Imran's question felt like a slap across her face.

A couple of other people were also standing around the canteen and chatting. The tea sitting in front of Niloufer was getting cold. She was sitting stock-still, trying to think of what to say to him. Her headscarf was fluttering in the breeze.

'Your tea is getting cold. Drink it,' he said, pulling her out of her thoughts.

'Hmmm, I will,' she said and picked up the cup. 'She has already converted to Islam … then why won't your village and family accept her?' she asked sadly. The helplessness in her voice made Imran's firm resolve shake a little.

'My village is nothing like you might know. We live a life of honour and pride and enjoy a high status; I don't want to cause any rifts in the family. It's not just that. Love is not like alms. For a person with her education and social status, she is sure to find a better partner than me. She won't fit into my way of life and with my family. Please ask her to forget about all of this.'

Niloufer's heart was pained by the sight of him pleading with her this way in his trembling voice.

'I understand everything, except for one. The fact that she has converted to Islam should suffice to get your family's approval or to announce to your village. Bringing a girl from another religion into the fold of Islam means ensuring a place for yourself in Heaven, isn't it?' she muttered under her breath. 'Okay, I'm leaving now. It's getting dark,' she got up and began to drag her short and slightly plump body away wearily. She was tormented by a relentless despair.

It was getting late for maghrib prayer. He unfolded the cap in his hand and wore it on his head.

35

'CONGRATS!' IMRAN SHOOK ANITHA'S EXTENDED HAND and hugged her.

'You're the only one who passed the campus interview and landed a job in our gang, da!' Dhana slapped Imran on his back.

'There is no need for you to work a job. They won't let you at home,' Imran said jokingly to Niloufer. A faint trace of sadness appeared in her face. 'I'll be going to an IT company in Mumbai. You are all going in different directions,' Imran laughed.

'Yes, of course ... I will be getting married and going to Dubai. You, da?' Niloufer asked, looking at Dhana.

'I will look for a job, what else?'

Everyone turned their attention to Anitha now.

'My family is looking for a groom for me. If I had got selected through the campus interview, I thought I could put off getting married for a year using work as an excuse. Now they will not allow me to wander in search for a job,' she was crestfallen.

Imran chimed in, 'Why don't you seek their permission to prepare for IAS exams? You can say you want to join classes in Chennai or Kerala and postpone marriage by two years!'

'That's a great idea!' Dhana and Niloufer cried in unison. Imran stroked his small beard absentmindedly, lost in thought. A very deep sigh escaped him. *Two years is a long time.* He finally said, 'Turn to Allah and it will happen. Inshallah.' Anitha and the others nodded in agreement. 'Now, you start looking for a way to get permission from your family. I will look for a good coaching centre for you. That is my responsibility,' Imran declared.

Niloufer and Anitha concurred with '*Ameen*'.

Anitha and Imran's love for each other had grown steadfast, which pleased Niloufer. When Anitha's father had been killed in a plane crash on his way back home from the Gulf, Imran had showed her kindness as he never had before. After the loss of her father, she had turned into a living corpse. He had admitted to his love and affection for her, which gave her hope. If she had not been struck with such tragedy, Niloufer was certain Imran would have rejected her.

He arranged for her to be enrolled at a centre in Thiruvananthapuram and took care to settle her into her accommodation before heading back to Mumbai. On the way to the airport, Anitha held both his hands and said, 'Thank you for everything, da.' He had found this centre from a friend, paid her fees, found her a place to stay through a friend's sister and painstakingly ensured all arrangements were in place so she didn't have to worry about anything except her studies, and she was grateful to him for all of it. He shrugged it off as though he hadn't done anything at all and took his leave.

As he got into his car, he said, 'After you become an IAS officer, please don't forget me, madam,' with a wink and a smile.

'Pch ... Stop it, Imran. You're always messing around. Here I am already yearning to see you again. I'm going to miss you,' she said, bidding him goodbye.

36

WHEN ANITHA FAILED HER FIRST ATTEMPT AT THE IAS examination, Imran went to see her in person to comfort her. He went directly from the airport to her accommodation to pick her up and called her on her mobile. 'I am here in the car, are you coming?'

'I'll be right there,' she said and within the next few seconds, was downstairs wearing a smile. 'Hi … How are you?' she said. He noticed her voice and her actions felt rather put on. 'Drive quickly now, or someone will see us. There's a lot of moral policing in Kerala.'

'Oh yes!' he said and started driving. 'If your friends are around, I thought I'd say hello to them too.'

'They are all in the room. But they don't know that we're in love. If they come to know I love a Muslim boy, they will start acting weirdly.'

'But will they not come to know when we get married?'

'We will find a way to manage it when that happens.'

Imran turned to look at her face. Expecting to find her upset from failing her exam and hoping that he would be able to offer her support, he was bewildered by her nonchalance.

'I'm hungry, shall we go to a restaurant? I woke up really early to catch my flight, and I didn't eat anything on the flight either.'

'Of course, let's eat. There, you can stop at that hotel, it's good.'

Just as he was going to stop the car, she apprised him, 'Do you still eat only halal food? They don't serve halal here.'

Her callousness shocked him. 'You're behaving as though you know nothing about me,' he said and began driving again.

Only then did he notice that she was wearing a bindi on her forehead and a sleeveless top. She had just brushed away the hair from her face and revealed her forehead. He was gripped with panic, although he continued to drive quietly. She was fully absorbed in her mobile. Unlike Mumbai, the roads in Thiruvananthapuram were not crowded, which aided his measured driving. The words caught in his throat made him gasp for breath. He stopped in front of Malappuram restaurant, parked the car and got out.

'A Muslim hotel!' she remarked, laughing. He noticed a difference in her laugh. He didn't say anything about it then and quietly entered the hotel. He imagined his silence silenced her too. She followed him in.

He looked around and found a table in a corner. He ordered a parotta and beef curry.

'I will get fish, please. I don't want beef.'

He thought he heard her lay special emphasis on the 'beef', but ignored it. He came directly to his point: 'What are you going to do next, are you going to try again?'

'No, no. I'm planning to prepare for the Intelligence Bureau exam now.'

He was so used to them making decisions together that he found it rather strange and surprising that she had made a decision on her own and was now stating it to him so matter-of-factly.

Maybe her self-confidence has been boosted by all this change and that's why she's making all these decisions for her future by herself, he speculated. *It's good. From now on, I won't have to sit in Mumbai and worry about her being alone and struggling by herself here.*

'Have you told the people at home yet? What did they say?' he asked.

'They've agreed to it,' she said casually, even as he was left feeling horrified.

'Oh … so I'm the last one to know.' His voice lowered as he spoke.

'Is that your ego? We were going to meet in person, so I decided to wait until now to tell you. Don't act this way, da,' she said and burst out laughing. Her loud laughter must have made the people around them turn and look at them.

Imran noticed a young man sitting at the table next to theirs, dressed in a black shirt and veshti, looking at them judgmentally. His bulky body, unkempt beard and a moustache that was turned just a hint upwards at the ends scared him a little. He didn't seem to care that Imran was looking back at him. His gaze travelled back and forth between them and his food.

Imran got very suspicious. He pinched himself to ascertain that he was indeed sitting opposite Anitha and not someone else. Is this the same girl he had known and spent four years with? Could she really have changed so much in just one year? He was dumbfounded. Their food was served and Imran could see a thousand questions lurking behind the eyes of the lean waiter who had brought them their food. He ignored the look and they began eating.

'Does your family know that we are in love?' he asked.

She didn't seem to like that question. She put the idli that she had picked up back onto the plate, lifted her head slowly and looked at him sharply. 'I haven't mentioned it to them as yet. I think amma knows. When she asks me about it, I'll tell her.' He observed that she was speaking faster than she used to.

Imran was suddenly reminded of Vinutha. When she had expressed her interest in him as they had been leaving their workplace the previous evening, he had told her in response about Anitha. He remembered how her face had shrunk with disappointment.

Anitha noticed that a couple of other diners were looking at them and eavesdropping on their conversation. 'Eat quickly, let's talk on the way,' she said, rushing him. 'In Kerala, they just stare shamelessly at everyone like this,' Anitha sounded irritated.

He suddenly realized that she still hadn't asked him even once how he was doing or how his work was going; that she wasn't really paying attention to him at all. He felt frazzled by it. *Has she really changed? What could be the reason behind it? Why is she so distant?* Imran struggled to understand what was going on. Was it time that had created this wide chasm between them? It perplexed him. He did not know what to say and drove on quietly. Because they had no particular place in mind to go to, he kept driving wherever he wished.

'Our state is not like Chennai. Everybody stares openly. Only on paper this state has 100 per cent literacy. The way the women stare is downright obnoxious,' Anitha said wearily. 'How are you? You look the same. You haven't changed one bit. Looks like even Mumbai couldn't change you … how sad,' she teased him.

'What do you mean by "change"? Should I change my character in some way? Or should I change my appearance? Should I maybe change my culture? Or should I change as you have?' His deadpan voice and his tone must have unnerved her. Perhaps it even hurt her. He panted for breath, getting worked up. She just sat quietly, looking out of her window at the streets for a little while. She seemed determined not to give him an answer.

He got angry with himself. Realizing that he must have upset her, he grabbed her right hand and said 'I'm sorry, dear …' She tried to free her hand forcefully. Her long, polished nails scratched him slightly.

'Aah!' he cried and let go of her hand. Only then did he notice her long nails, polished immaculately. Growing one's nails and putting polish on them was *makrooh*; he remembered she had told him a long time ago that it was forbidden by Islam to keep them this way during prayers. He didn't want to think about those days, but they did scratch their way into his mind sporadically.

It was a good thing that she had changed and although he had no qualms about, he was troubled by the thought that maybe he lacked the maturity to accept this change. *Maybe, like she pointed out, it is me who hasn't changed even a bit. If this change in her was brought about by her environment, what right do I have to find fault with it?*

It was futile to wonder why these changes hadn't come about when they had been studying together for four years. Back then, she had accepted his beliefs for his sake. Maybe she did not feel the need to accept all of his beliefs any longer. *Things are not the same as they used to be back then. She would have understood that the world is much bigger than what we knew. There's nothing for me to worry about.*

Her silence still hung heavy in the air between them. He felt like a stranger to himself. The heat outside had mellowed. They decided to walk around on the streets. The intense heat of the concrete under their feet felt like an inferno growing within him and worsening his feeling of dejection. He was confused about what to do and where to go next. He had so many things to say, to share with her. Yet, his loneliness and emptiness had silenced him. She did not seem to have anything to say or share with him either.

He felt cheated. He wanted to say something to escape the silence. 'So, madam, where should we go now? Won't you at least tell me that? You are from here and I'm new to the place,' he said, forcing a laugh.

'Let's go to the beach,' she said, following it with a faint smile. He would be able to catch his flight in time from there. 'Let's go to one of the beaches in the outskirts, closer to the airport. I'll tell you the way,' she said. 'You're upset with me, aren't you? That my whole demeanour – with the sleeveless top, unbraided hair, bindi, nails, nail polish – has completely changed. Earlier, when I was with you, I didn't do any of this because I thought you wouldn't approve of it. I had changed my religion. But I'm not like that anymore. I wear whatever I feel like wearing.

'I don't pray anymore either. It's not that I have changed, it's more like I'm returning to my old self. I'm sorry, but it's not like I have forgotten you.' She spoke with clarity.

Imran understood the reality and wanted to accept her just as she was. In a corner of his heart, he knew that their love had strayed very far from any possibility of marriage. *It's not wrong for her to dislike the world I live in; who am I to try and change her mind?* As soon as he seemed to understand this, Anitha's face lit up.

He took both her hands in his and squeezed them to express his love for her. She smiled in acknowledgement.

37

'WHEN DID YOU GET BACK FROM KERALA, IMRAN?' Vinutha Sagar asked him, squeezing his shoulders and bringing him back to the present.

It was only then that he realized he was in his office.

'Hi Vinu, I came back last night.'

'How was Kerala? How is your girlfriend?' she asked enthusiastically.

'Yeah … she is fine. Kerala too,' he said and smiled.

Vinutha's face brightened. 'I wanted to come with you but you didn't tell me in time.'

He opened the package on his desk and brought out a Kerala-style sari from it that he had bought at the airport.

'Is this for me? Thank you! I don't know how to drape a sari, but I will certainly wear it one day.' She thanked him in Tamil, English and Kannada and laughed. Her hair cascaded over her broad shoulders and danced in sync with her words; it was a beautiful sight.

'Presenting you with a sari when you don't know how to drape one is akin to giving a toothless man a kalkona candy, am I right, da?' Murugan, who sat at the workstation next to theirs, teased him. Vinutha looked clueless about what Murugan had said to him in Tamil and Imran laughed without replying to him. Their laughter was infectious, rippling across the office.

Nowadays, whenever Vinutha enquired about Anitha or her progress preparing for the exam, Imran felt as if she was driven by guilt, although he never said that to her.

'Tonight is Meghna's birthday party, why don't you come along?' Vinutha asked. Even though they were all colleagues, he did not usually participate in such merriment. Everyone would drink on the occasion and he was a teetotaler.

'I won't be able to come … I'm tired.'

'No one will insist that you drink. Please come? Meghna won't spare you if you don't agree,' she said with a wink and gestured to Meghna, who was standing a little away from them, to come on over.

'Yes, darling,' she said, walking over to them, 'you have to come. Madras Boy, there will be beef, grilled chicken and fresh juice there. I can't let you skip.' She tapped him lightly on his face.

Knowing he couldn't decline the invitation anymore, Imran acquiesced and nodded.

'Oh great!' the two women exclaimed, grabbing hold of both his hands and shaking them in jubilation. Even though Imran was shy, he didn't try to stop them. He kept quiet to avoid engaging with them further so they would leave him be.

'In the whole world, if there was only one person whom God loves and watches over all the time, do you know who that would be? Our Imran, of course! He monitors him all the time, working overtime. He doesn't look anywhere else even for a moment,' his colleagues would gang up on him and pull his leg. Not wanting to give them more opportunities to do so, he simply relented.

'How is it that God is always fixating on you all the time, da? Wouldn't he get bored only ever monitoring you?' they would tease him in all sorts of ways. He never got upset; he just smiled and let it go.

Vinutha said, 'Let's go together tonight. I will come over to your place and we can take your car. We need a designated driver.'

'Done!' Imran agreed.

The loud music, laughter and cigarette smoke which made Imran cough until his throat hurt … His friends couldn't seem to stop drinking. It was impossible to hear anything over the noise. With a glass of wine in her hand, Vinutha came and sat next to him. The two had a lot to talk about by themselves.

'These days you've been coming to the weekend parties week after week without us having to coax you. What has happened to you?' he suddenly remembered Vinutha had asked him just that morning. 'What are you thinking about, Imran?' She interrupted his thoughts now, holding him by his shoulders and shaking him.

'Nothing …' he smiled. He wondered if he should tell her about his conversation with Anitha over the phone. Vinutha sensed he wanted to say something to her and said, 'Come, let's go outside,' opening the door closest to her to exit the club. Geoffrey's Pub was very popular and very crowded. Imran followed her outside. The noise was muffled by the glass doors shutting behind them. Freeing his ears from the grips of the tortuous clamour made him feel at ease.

'All this noise … I'm not used to it at all,' he said, shrugging his shoulders to emphasize his discomfort.

'Yes, it is all about getting used to. Don't worry about it.'

He looked up at Vinutha trying to comfort him. In her black party dress, she shone like a wax doll. A cool breeze caressed him. Scattered around them, a couple of lovers were drinking and chatting. Noticing him staring at her she asked him, surprised, 'Why, what happened, mister? You are looking at me so intently.'

Even though he wanted to respond to her right away, he stayed quiet as if he needed some time. Vinutha waited for his silence to fade of its own accord.

'I feel like my interactions with Anitha have changed a lot. It's really hard.' He started talking suddenly and then hung his head in silence.

'Oh! I see … What happened?'

'She started saying certain things as if she were teasing me, but it feels like she's ridiculing me. She's nothing like she used to be. She doesn't follow Islam. Last time, when I met her in person, I was rather shocked, but I didn't want to make a big deal out of it. I can't live without her … I love her so much. I have tried thousands of times to use my religious beliefs as an excuse to part ways with her. But since my heart doesn't seem to agree, I don't think I can make religion an issue between us. Lately, she's been saying things like "Muslim youngsters practise love *jihad* and it is wrong". She even supports Modi! I've noticed a huge change in her behaviour. The term "love jihad" has only been popularized recently by RSS – but we have been in a relationship for five years now and we certainly didn't plan any of this. Can either of us classify our true love like this? It's just nonsense!' Imran poured his heart out in a single breath. His already angry face had now flushed blood red.

Vinutha noticed the tip of his sharp nose twitching. She gently placed her hands around his shoulders and pacified him. 'Don't overreact, please. The fact that Anitha has bought into the state propaganda is quite shocking, yes, but it could just have had something to do with her current frame of mind. You cannot let that spill into your relationship. You shouldn't even think this way.'

He was not in the mood to listen to her, but he kept quiet. He felt flustered thinking about how he may have revealed his vulnerable side to her.

'Whoever she chooses to support – BJP or Modi –

isn't that her own individual right? What's your problem with that? What does your love for her have to do with it?'

Imran believed Anitha was provoking him. He could not look at it any other way.

'I also cannot just forget BJP, or Modi, or the riots in Gujarat. But how can I let any of that have an impact on my personal life, tell me?'

He paused, looking for an answer to her question.

'What are you guys doing here outside?' Vikas came looking for them, and that made them turn their attention away from their conversation.

'Nothing, Vikas,' Vinutha replied quickly.

'Okay, then let's go back in,' Vikas said, lighting a cigarette.

The two of them realized that it was the right thing to do and followed Vikas inside. Even though Vinutha wanted to stay outside and keep talking to Imran, she had no choice but to join them. Vikas paused for a second, looked at the fruit juice in Imran's hand and teased him, laughing, 'When are you going to change, da?'

Not just his voice but his body too was unsteady, Imran noticed.

'Get over it, man. Let him be the way he wants to be,' Vinutha scolded Vikas with a laugh.

She got out of Imran's car as they pulled up in front of her apartment. 'Goodnight ... get some sleep. Let's talk over the phone tomorrow,' she said and waved to him.

Over the next few days, she talked to him as many times as it took to help him understand and settle his differences with Anitha. Imran was truly astounded. He reflected on how even after she had confessed her love for him and he had turned her down, she carried herself with grace and remained sincerely concerned for Anitha. He felt ashamed at his own lack of composure.

38

WHEN VINUTHA CAME TO KNOW THAT ANITHA HAD passed the Intelligence Bureau exam, she congratulated Imran profusely. She was even happier to learn that he was personally accompanying her to Delhi for her training. She enthusiastically made all arrangements – from their respective flights from Mumbai and Kerala so they could meet at the airport and head over together to Vinutha's brother's place in Vasant Vihar, to how he would spend the two days he was there before he returned after dropping her off at her training centre.

'We could have stayed at a hotel. Why should we stay at your friend's brother's place?' Anitha sulked.

'You're new to Delhi. It would be good for you to know somebody there in case of an emergency,' Imran had replied.

Even though Anitha did not care much for the arrangement, she saw how Ravi Halkare and his wife Kruti were so warm towards them and conceded. 'Not bad, might actually be nice to be friends with them,' she said, appreciating them.

They made a day trip to Taj Mahal and Fatehpur Sikri. When she said she wanted to go to Mathura, Imran took her there. While she visited the temple to offer prayers, he walked around the streets. His head was clouded with confusion and he felt as if he'd been left to wander in a jungle without directions. His apprehensions about confronting his father, family and village were tearing him apart. What if he just disappeared – right here right this minute?

What can I do that could make my father look past all his concerns about prestige, respect and reputation and convince him to agree to our match? But can I even live happily with her? Will I just get over the huge differences between our religious beliefs because of how deeply I love her?

Anitha emerged from the temple with her forehead smeared with vermillion and *prasadam* in her hand. 'Come, let's go,' she said and he wondered if she too was grappling with the same worries as him. He noticed a few people standing outside the temple eyeing them both in disbelief before walking away.

As he was leaving her at the training centre, he held her hand and said, 'After your training is done, let's tell our families.' The saffron-coloured holy thread tied around her wrist bothered him.

'I told you my mother probably knows but she hasn't mentioned it to me as yet. Let her ask and we'll see.'

He did not miss her dismissive tone. *I'm okay if it happens and okay if it doesn't*, she seemed to be saying. While he hesitantly waved her goodbye, she seemed rather enthusiastic and full of hope taking her leave. He told himself that he was just being too imaginative, that such thoughts weren't going to bode well for him or Anitha. Realizing that helped him feel calmer.

39

TODAY WAS THE FIRST TIME NILOUFER HAD CALLED since she had got married, quite out of the blue.

'Hello lady! When did you fly in from Dubai?' Imran asked.

'Last week. He hasn't come along; it's just me. When will you come to visit?'

'I don't have anything else to do in Chennai. I'll have to come specially to see you. I'll come down next Sunday, okay? What else, how are you doing?'

'You're coming on Sunday? I will tell you then. You *must* come, okay?' she spoke quickly in excitement. 'I have another surprise for you: Anitha is coming too and I've also asked Dhanasekar. He lives in Chennai. So let's see!' She sounded more like she was issuing an order rather than an invitation.

'Anitha is coming?!' Imran was shocked. 'But her training is not yet over – is she flying in from Delhi? She didn't mention anything of the sort to me.'

'Dei, don't get angry, da. She will tell you. Let her come first!' Niloufer laughed.

He talked to her for a little while before hanging up

the phone, confused. For no reason at all, he gazed at his mobile. *She still hasn't told me. Niloufer's voice wasn't as cheery and teasing as it used to be. She sounded like she called me only because she had to.* He turned his attention back to his work.

As expected, he got a call from Anitha that night. 'I'm coming to Chennai. I want to see Niloufer. You should come too. I need to talk to you as well – it's about our future,' she said decisively. There was no frenzy in her voice, she sounded extra clear and confident, he noticed with surprise.

'What? You want to talk about the future? That's funny. We talk every day; what are we going to talk about the future now that we haven't already discussed? Why don't you meet with Niloufer and go back. I am a little busy with work, I'll just come to Delhi next week.'

'No, Imran,' Anitha immediately declined his suggestion. 'The four of us need to be together to talk and make some decisions. You *have* to come.' This time her statement sounded more like an order. He was unsettled by the striking change in her tone from what he was used to. Her tone made it plain that he had no choice but to listen to her. He disliked being treated this way, but he agreed to go nevertheless. There was no room to refuse. He felt something break within him.

By the time they met at Coffee Day in Nungambakkam, it had already begun getting dark. Dhana and Imran arrived directly from Dhana's accommodation. The Coffee Day was very close to Niloufer's place. Dhana was greatly confused. 'What is going on, da?' he tried asking Imran over and over again. He dodged his question because he didn't have an answer.

Was there an issue at Anitha's house? Was her family planning to get her married to someone else? He was himself unsure about what was going on. He knew, however, that they could not arrive at a decision based on mere assumption. The café wasn't crowded and felt comfortable. A couple was sitting at a table by the window. The woman was dressed in highly fashionable clothing and her demeanour reminded Imran of Vinutha. Her dress was up to her thighs and he could see her legs.

'Hello!' Niloufer's voice rang out; they both turned around. She was with Anitha and they had already approached the table. 'What were you thinking about that you didn't even notice we'd arrived?' she teased Imran.

'Hi Dhana, hi Imran,' Anitha came closer to them and placed her hands on both their shoulders.

'Come, come, Miss IB officer! Can I shake your hand or should I be saluting you?' Dhanasekar joked as he shook her hand. 'And you shouldn't have got this fat, aunty,' he said, pulling Niloufer's leg.

Niloufer had visibly put on weight. Living abroad,

the different food, climate and new family relationships – her life had changed drastically and its impact showed on her body. Anitha sat across from Imran. She was wearing a black salwar set and a matching black stick-on bindi on her forehead. Dhana seemed bewildered by her appearance.

The four friends sat in a private area that had been reserved for them. 'I'm pregnant. Five months in. That's why I've come. Anwar hasn't come; he just sent me over. He'll come in time for the delivery. Okay, so shall we place our order now?' Niloufer said, picking up the menu.

Anitha said, 'Order an almond smoothie for me, please.'

After they had all made their selections and conveyed them to the waiter serving them, Dhana teased Anitha, 'So, looks like you've become thin and tan from eating chapatis in Delhi!'

'Oh stop … try living there, then you will know. The heat and then the cold … You won't last a day there, you sack of rice!'

She seemed rather overwhelmed with hesitation before she went on. 'First, I want to apologize to the three of you. In the last year that I've been living away from Imran, my worldview has changed dramatically. I know I converted to Islam for him and did everything for him in accordance with his religion. It wasn't even very difficult back then. But now I'm beginning to believe that I can't live like that anymore. I'm over those things. I've understood and accepted that I can't fit into his world. I've started believing more strongly now that I'm my own independent person. I want to live for myself first; this is my life. Whether this shift in my mindset is right or wrong, I can't tell, but to marry a Muslim boy without believing in his religion; to try and fit into his lifestyle … it's just not something I think I can do. I believe it would be best if we just part ways and remain the great friends we already are. That's why I asked you all to come so I could tell everyone in person.' Anitha concluded and looked down quietly. Her accent had a lot more Malayalam flavour than before. Niloufer, who bore a look of surprise at the beginning of her speech was filled with anger by the time she finished.

Dhana exploded, 'Ey … do you even realize what you're saying? Or have you lost your mind?'

Niloufer noticed Imran crumbling to rubble within. 'Ey, you fraud – what are you saying?! And who are you even saying all this to? Has your education made you so conceited?' her voice got uncharacteristically louder.

Dhana fumbled with his words in anger. 'Isn't he the reason you could even get this education? How can you even think of just using him and then cutting him off like this? Is your relationship really that disposable? Shit!' He was yelling now.

The exchanges around him brought Imran back to his senses. He had been expecting this. Perhaps the distance he had been feeling between them lately had been building up to this moment. Even though what she had meant to say was rather simple, it was how she had said it and the words she had used that had agitated him. 'Please ... calm down, Nilo and Dhana,' he finally said. His loud, firm voice quietened them immediately. 'She has taken a decision and she has come to it entirely on *her own*. To shout at her expecting things to carry on like before is not right,' he said. His emphasis on 'her own' was a rather thinly veiled accusation.

'You stay quiet, da. I'll talk sense into her,' Dhana snapped. His heavy frame was still trembling with anger. 'What are you trying to say, Anitha? That he tricked you into falling in love with him? Or that he's not fit to live with you? Why don't you just admit that you used him, finished your studies and now you're washing your hands of him,' his anger flashed in his eyes.

The words 'used him' must have affected Anitha severely. She cut him off coldly with 'Shut up, Dhana. You better watch your language.' Her voice was shaking too.

'Madam, please don't get angry. You have no right to. Who do you think you are asking to mind their language? *You* stalked *him* until he gave in; not the other way round. We know exactly what happened,' Niloufer burst out. Her red face and her even deeper red ears throbbed. The two seemed to be plagued with guilt from having played a role in pushing for this relationship.

Imran realized that the situation was getting out of hand. 'Nilo, Dhana, please keep quiet,' he tried to constrain them.

The young man who was carrying their order approached them uncertainly, placed the drinks on their table, looked at their faces and left.

Anitha's face darkened. 'You don't need to blame me. I shared how I feel. I'm an IB officer now. My life, my work, everything is going to look very different. His life and his lifestyle are completely different. I believe it would be best for me to marry someone from my field. I am telling you this now because I don't want the two of us to get married and then go through all this trouble later when we realize we are just not right for each other. Try to understand. I know Imran, he'll understand.'

Niloufer immediately put two and two together. 'Oh! So then why don't you just admit that you already have someone else in mind? Why are you hiding that information?'

'Yes, I do,' Anitha admitted confidently as if she had been waiting for this moment all along. 'I like Arun Agarwal, who is training with me. Based on the time we've spent together, I think we are quite compatible and that's why I'm thinking about getting married to him. I've already told my mother. Same type of work, same religion, same level of education – I don't believe there will be any issues.'

Her body language made it clear that she felt no

remorse, so no one had anything more to say. A heavy silence hung over them.

'Don't you feel any guilt at all?' Niloufer asked her in a low voice.

'What do you want me to feel guilty about? I loved him then, spent some time together but now, in my current state of mind, I feel like I won't be able to live with him and that we are not right for each other. Isn't this a good thing? Instead of getting married and dealing with these problems later, isn't it better that we part ways now?'

Imran's eyes were welling up. His mind struggled to accept that a person who had loved him with all her heart was now simply casting him aside. He was overwhelmed and tried hard to maintain his composure. He hung his head in humiliation. He had never felt this great a disappointment in his life before and was deeply hurt. For a person who had never cried until then, he wanted to break down; he controlled himself with immense difficulty. All he wanted was to lie in his kuppi's lap and let it all out.

'If I had told him when we were alone, he would have felt really bad. That's why I asked you all to come. Please try and understand; don't get mad at me.'

Everyone's hearts were flaming hot; the coffees placed in front of them had grown cold.

'Okay, let's leave then,' Niloufer said curtly and got up to leave. It was only then that Imran noticed that her belly really was showing. *Is this really Niloufer? Who knew she was capable of such anger?* Imran and Dhana stared at her in shock. 'Imran, Dhana, I'm going to pay and leave. We'll meet tomorrow,' she said and left.

Anitha too got up, bid them goodbye and left. That farewell was rather casual. A simple goodbye that carried neither pain nor guilt.

Imran could not even register her goodbye, let alone respond to it. He could feel nothing at all. Dhana held his friend's hand and stayed still. Watching the lights from the vehicles passing by on the road and the people walking on the street from inside the café, Imaran sat rooted to the spot, his face quivering with sorrow. He felt forced into a state of frailty, like he could shatter at any second.

Dhana realized it was best they left and returned to his room. He placed his hands on Imran's shoulder and shook him gently and said, 'Come, let's leave.'

Imran stood up snapping out of his daze. Dhana wrapped his arm over his shoulders and gave him a hug. They slowly walked towards Dhana's car. 'Bloody woman ... how selfish—' Dhana had more to say, but Imran interrupted him with 'Please, Dhana ...' to calm him down.

Once the car was in motion, Imran covered his face with his hands and burst into sobs. Streams of his tears wet his youthful stubble.

What an amazing person he is. He's always attentive to

the needs of his friends and would not hesitate to bend over backwards to help them out. Dhanasekar's anger amplified thinking of the Anitha's great betrayal of such a man. When Imran was vehemently opposed to a relationship, it was he and Niloufer who had tormented him incessantly until he had given in. The thought that the blame for all this lay with himself and Niloufer unsettled him deeply; a tremor ran down his spine. He started driving faster. Who else was to take responsibility for how things had turned out but himself?

His cellphone rang. He picked up and asked, 'Niloufer, have you reached home?'

'Yes, I've reached home. Anitha said she was going to her aunt's place and has left. How's he doing?' she asked gingerly.

'He's with me. We are on our way to my room. I'll talk to you later,' his voice sounded dry.

When Anitha's father had died in an airplane accident, Imran had been in his hometown. Dhanasekar and Niloufer had been by Anitha's side, trying to console her. As soon as Dhana called Imran on his cellphone to let him know what had happened, he arranged for the three of them to fly to Kozhikode. Once all the rites were done and he and Niloufer had returned to college, Dhana felt very troubled. His mind was tormented by Anitha's family situation, her and her mother's helplessness and the larger questions about whether she would be able to continue her education.

During their return journey, Niloufer didn't speak a word. Since he didn't want to go to class, Dhana went to the canteen instead. It was before noon, the sun was beating down hard. He sat at a table in a corner with his legs outstretched, deep in thought. The smell of coffee and the aroma wafting from the sandwiches made him hungry. He hadn't eaten anything since the previous day.

'What are you doing sitting here?' He turned around hearing the voice. Imran was standing there.

'Nothing, sit down,' he said to him.

'How's Anitha?' Imran asked. 'Poor thing, fate really did her in.'

'Pch, their family is in a very sad state, da, at least you shouldn't have left her in the lurch,' Dhana said, suddenly grabbing Imran's hands.

Imran frowned in confusion at what he implied.

'A girl falling in love with you and converting to your religion is not an easy thing to find, da. Do you know how much pain you're causing her by ignoring her? If you cannot understand a girl's heart, what are you even hoping to achieve with just your education?'

'What am I to do about that? Let her study and stand on her own two feet,' Imran replied sternly.

'Who will support her education going forward? It's just not going to happen. I don't think she's ever coming back here again. You can live peacefully now.'

'Why won't she?'

'She's not planning to pursue her studies further – her circumstances don't support it. But more importantly, I don't know how she's going to go on without you.'

Imran understood what Dhana meant and kept quiet. The sun was directly above them, in the middle of the sky, radiating heat mercilessly all around. A breeze blowing through the neem tree tried to alleviate the heat in some measure.

'Love is not what we think and understand it to be; guys like you will never get it,' Dhana declared.

Imran was very perturbed.

'Okay, I'm going to leave now. You can go for your prayers, it's time,' Dhana said.

In the days that had followed, when Anitha had not returned to college, Imran had undergone a change of heart. Bringing her back to college had been his way of accepting her.

Dhana snapped out of his thoughts. His guilt gnawed at him. He couldn't find a way to comfort the pain that had seized Imran's fragile heart.

'Take care of him, he seems so broken. She has turned into the epitome of selfishness. I want nothing to do with her anymore, bloody …' Niloufer gnashed her teeth. Dhana found Niloufer's anger surprising since she was always in such good spirits, as though she knew no other emotion but joy. He was shocked to see her get so mad.

'Okay, hang up now. We'll talk later,' he said and ended the call short.

He drove along the beach road. The beach was crowded. He checked the time – it wasn't yet ten. He parked the car in a less crowded area, grabbed Imran by his shoulders and hugged him.

'Dei, why are you crying? She's not worthy of you. She pinned the blame on you, of all people, and washed her hands of you. Forget her, fool.' Dhana tried to console his friend. The sea breeze caressed their faces momentarily and slipped away. He felt disappointment and bitterness like never before.

For the first time, Imran felt the pain of letting go of something that he had desired with all his heart. His father and his family had never inflicted such pain and dejection on him.

The dark, expansive ocean stretched out before them. Lovers strolled along the shores in places. Their laughter and togetherness made Imran uncomfortable. 'Let's go, da,' he said. It took a monumental effort for him to endure that long, sleepless night.

40

HE WAS ALREADY BACK IN HIS APARTMENT WHEN Vinutha asked him, 'Imran, where are you? Have you returned from Chennai?'

His head hurt and his body felt warm. 'Yeah, I came back yesterday itself. I'm feeling a little under the weather, I'm in my apartment.'

'What happened? Did you see a doctor? What did you eat?' she panicked.

'I had some bread. I just took medicine. Nothing to worry about, I'll be back in office tomorrow.'

'No, Imran. It's not a good idea for you to be alone right now. I'm coming over.' Giving him no chance to refuse, she hung up the phone.

He knew that if she came over, he would definitely crumble in front of her. But he knew there was no stopping her. He lay down, not knowing what to do.

He kept his apartment clean because he had to pray there five times a day and opted out of sharing an apartment with his friends. His was a single-bedroom apartment with a kitchen he had all to himself. Vinutha had visited him a few times before. 'Rich boy! You have an apartment to yourself in a posh neighbourhood. Live it up!' she would tease him.

He was supposed to go home to visit his father and mother, but because he had gone to Chennai instead, he hadn't been able to see them. Attha and amma had been very distraught. He had reassured them by promising to visit in the following week.

Unable to bear the rejection and the depression it had brought on, he had called Anitha's mother the previous night and yelled at her. 'How supportive I've been of your daughter all this time. I've loved her with everything I've got. She has betrayed me!'

Her mother too had yelled back at him. 'If my daughter doesn't want to be with you, then why won't you drop it? You keep saying you were in a relationship with her for five years and loved her, as if that means you have some kind of right over her. In the five years you were together, she may have grown to dislike something about you. That's probably why she came and talked to you about it. How is that betrayal or cheating? *Your kind* and *our kind* don't go together. Maybe that's why she made this decision. Now go away and stop bothering me – don't you dare try calling her either, I am warning you. Otherwise, I'll go to the police.' In her Tamil–Malayalam, she had yelled at him and called Niloufer right after.

Niloufer had exploded and severely berated her. 'Your daughter *chose* to convert, fast, pray and wear a burqah on her own. He didn't even think she was worth his time. It was me – I'm the fool who pushed him to accept her. He even paid her fees for the IAS exam, found her a place to live, settled her there … yes – he flew her there. Did you not know then – did *she* not know then that "your kind" and "his kind" don't go together? End this nonsense and put the phone down right now.'

When she told Imran all about it, he got very upset. 'Isn't gloating about the help we extend to others a terrible thing to do? You read the Qur'an, don't you? How could you forget its teachings and speak this way?' he chided her.

He had been in the doldrums all night for speaking so harshly to Niloufer thereafter. He turned the memories over and over in his mind – had he ever asked Anitha to convert or follow his faith or even spoken to her about religion at all? On one occasion, he had said to her, 'Whenever you visit my village, you will have to wear a burqah.' That too only because he didn't want to offend his attha right away or want his reputation in the village to suffer. *She too had agreed that it would be the right thing for her to do. Later, when she was in Kerala, she lived freely doing whatever she pleased. So, what happened?* He had been genuinely confused, and fallen asleep still feeling the sting of rejection.

He was roused by the sound of his doorbell and got up to open the door. Vinutha was standing there. 'Why couldn't you tell me that you weren't feeling well? Would I not have come over to help?' she said angrily. She placed the fruits she had got for him on the table and put her hand to his forehead. 'You have a fever. Wait, I'll get you some hot water. You can take your medicine too,' she said, walking into the kitchen.

Imran was wearing just his baniyan and felt a little shy. He quickly threw on the T-shirt on a hanger nearby and lay down. He was tired. The exhaustion of his weary heart was affecting the rest of his body as well. The anger bubbling within, the helplessness, sadness, resentment – everything was weighing down heavy on him.

He knew Vinutha was going to ask him about his trip to Chennai. It would not be possible for him to hide anything from her either. Above all else, he thought about how he had rejected her by telling her he was with Anitha when she had professed her love to him. The fact that today that very Anitha had left him was mortifying. As he fretted about how he was going to tell Vinutha about it all, his gloom balled up in his throat and choked him.

'Here, take this medicine and I will make you some porridge for lunch. Lie down and sleep off now. You don't need to worry about me doing all this. I can cook just fine,' she said and laughed.

Imran took his medicine and thanked her. She was wearing jeans and a kurta. When she went to parties, she usually wore crop tops and skirts. He was surprised at how the modern woman that he knew her to be was here, making porridge for him. He shut his eyes and drifted into sleep.

When he woke up, he found Vinutha waiting. 'It's dark out, I should leave. I'll come back tomorrow morning. Here, drink this juice,' she said and let herself out.

She had swept and cleaned his apartment, washed the utensils, cleaned the kitchen, washed his clothes in the washing machine and hung them to dry and made kanji and thuvayal for him. He was astonished at how responsible she had been. It made him wonder if the girl who was always joking around, teasing everyone and laughing at work was the same as the one he had seen today. Above all, he was deeply moved by the love and care she had displayed for him. *In the moments I spend with her, why am I reminded of amma and kuppi?* Of course, it was because she looked after him with the same affection as them. He felt ashamed of how he had known her all these days but had only ever thought of her as a party animal. His realization that she possessed such a capacity to love others began to turn into respect for her.

'Vinu, I need to talk to you,' he told her when she arrived the next morning.

'What is it?' she asked, placing her bag on the sofa and sitting close to him. He took her hands in his and burst into tears. Like a small, helpless baby, his whole body shook as he cried.

The pride that had blinded him to the selfless love of the woman sitting in front of him was pulverized. All the emotions that were making him suffer on the inside now overflowed from his heart and onto her. His tears, like unending pleas pouring out of a jilted heart, found shelter on Vinutha's shoulders.

Vinutha tried to console him patiently, but it was in vain. She started crying too. A long silence hung in the air between them. 'Well, what are you going to do now? Forget about her or sit here and cry thinking about it?' Vinutha asked as she wiped the tears off his sharp nose and looked straight into his eyes.

Imran noticed how natural her question felt. He had arrived at a clear decision. He knew it was foolish to cry a river over someone who had broken his heart so thoughtlessly. It was Vinutha's extraordinary words and actions that had birthed the thoughts which had led him here. *How was she so strong?* He sat quietly, not letting her in on his silent admiration of her. Faced with the strong-willed woman, the flustered man decided it would be best for him to hide his cowardice from her.

'Why would I think of her again? No more. It will take me a few days, but I'll be alright,' he mumbled absentmindedly. His frown revealed the conflict within.

'Okay, I'll stay the night. You can sleep peacefully. Even if I go home, I will keep worrying about you and won't be able to rest.'

He looked at her in shock. How had she made that decision so suddenly? 'No, no, you can go. There's nothing to worry about,' he tried to deter her.

'Pch ... you keep quiet, da,' she silenced him with just that. 'I'll sleep on the sofa in the living room. No more discussions on the topic.' She did not wait for him to react.

Although he was left sitting there in shock, he felt happy she was staying the night. He knew it would have been impossibly hard for him to get through the night by himself and felt great relief. His face expressed his approval to her. For the moment, that seemed enough.

41

VINUTHA TOOK ANITHA'S PHONE NUMBER FROM IMRAN and called her up. On the one hand, she was worried about Imran and on the other, she was relieved it was going to be over for good. *Still, it might be worth calling Anitha and finding out what her problem with him really is.* She wasn't sure if it was the right thing to do. What was with her need to talk to someone she had never met or spoken to in the past? Her mind wavered as the phone rang on the other end until it stopped.

She heaved a sigh of relief when Anitha did not answer. *Why am I so agitated?* she wondered and wished she hadn't called. *In less than a minute, I would have exposed Imran's disappointment*, she reproached herself. *Why didn't I think about how it would have made him feel even worse? I was going to do something so foolish! What will I say to Anitha if she calls back?* she wondered. *That won't be so difficult to handle*, she decided, and went about her work.

Imran didn't come in to work that day. She had told him that he needn't until the following day.

42

WHEN VINUTHA CALLED, ANITHA WAS ON HER WAY to her hometown. Her mother and aunt had called her several times since the day before and cried to her. Even though the reason they wanted her to come immediately didn't really warrant her attention, she did feel compelled to go home right away. The journey from Delhi to Kozhikode by train was not the most convenient travel option, but it was the only one available at such short notice.

Why did Vinutha, who'd never spoken to me before, want to talk to me now? Why would she even think it possible?

Imran had once called her and introduced the two of them. Luckily for her, she had saved her number then. *Otherwise, I would have answered her call unknowingly and said something to her. That call was bound to get awkward and lead to more complications.* Her thoughts drifted to an event from six months ago. Her mother's distraught voice deep into that night rang in her ears even now.

'Your aunt's daughter has eloped with that boy! You have to come home immediately, mole.' Because of the panic in her voice, Anitha had set out on her journey with great anxiety.

She was furious at her cousin Kavya, who was as close to her as a younger sister. *How many times do I have to advise her not to trust guys!*

Initially, her mother had told her that Kavya was in love with Faisal, the son of the owner of a stationery store at the end of their street. 'Drill some sense into her. She talks to that Faisal all the time, it makes me nervous.' Anitha was taken aback by the news. *What is going on?* she wondered. *How can I ask her not to do this when I'm doing the same thing?* The seeds of doubt about her life choices had been sown in her for the first time that day.

'In the last six months, three girls have abandoned their studies and eloped from our area. They have all run away with Muslim boys. Those sinners – they seem to be running this scheme like some kind of a business. I am very scared; there are no men in our family to look out for us,' her mother's sister had sobbed over the phone; she had been the one to console her.

Anitha took Kavya into a room so they could be alone and counselled her, 'You are only seventeen years old. There is so much you don't know about the world right now. Don't drift aimlessly with just anyone in the name of love.'

'Akka, nothing of that kind is going on, I swear on Lord Krishna. We only chat casually. He's my senior in college. I talk to him occasionally about the goings-on at college, nothing more. Don't you know how our family can get?' Kavya assured her. Beneath her light nightdress, Anitha could tell that her thin body was trembling with fear. Her face was slim and her eyes were set wide apart. 'We're just friends. It's only because his shop is right down the road that I end up talking to him. It's not like I go there looking for him.'

Anitha wanted to wipe the fear off her face and bring her back to her usual self.

'All that is okay. I understand. You are on the verge of finishing only your first year of college. Going around with strange men at such a time is the wrong call. You are going to college to study. Finishing your studies and earning a degree is your first order of business. Everything else comes after that. You understand?' She spoke very sternly to get her point across and then hugged her trembling little cousin.

She could tell that Kavya's head was in the clouds. One could see it in her face. 'Okay, I won't talk to him from now on,' she promised in her unsteady voice. Even though it seemed a tad too dramatic, Anitha had felt pressured to just take her at face value.

A few months later, she received the news that Kavya had eloped with the lad. Where was she to look for her; who was she to contact? Did it make sense to contact the police as yet? What would happen if the news reached others? Anitha's head was spinning with the endless questions.

Just then, the train crossed Kayangulam. There was still a long way to go.

Trusting someone you fell in love with as an adolescent and then being abandoned by them later is a very difficult situation for anyone to handle. Kavya has run away with that lad the day after she turned eighteen. Eloping with a girl before she finishes her studies and getting married is such a serious offence. If women don't even get to have an education, how can they possibly hope to take care of themselves during tough times? Just thinking about this was giving Anitha a headache. She was livid at the young man. She also realized she was moving closer to finally answering an unanswered question that had long stood before her.

Since the day Kavya had gone missing, the whole house had plunged into silence. Anitha's aunt was cowering with shame. She was anxious that they wouldn't be able to track her down before the news of her elopement spread. *What should we do now? What must be done? What can we do?* The words swirled around in her head repeatedly. When amma and her aunt started slapping their heads and crying, Anitha told them, 'We can't really do anything to them, so stop it.'

'Is it the arrogance from getting yourself an education that makes you say this?' amma screamed. She could not tolerate Anitha's apparent nonchalance. Her aunt, who was frozen in shock at her declaration, decided that she was going to be of no help and proceeded to call her husband's younger brother. Anitha did not stop her.

Krishnan Nair, who lived two streets away, came running in a frenzy. His demeanour and language oozed an overzealousness from finally finding the opportunity to bring their patriarch-less family under his control after so many years of lying in wait. Anitha found that disgusting.

'How can you just let something like this slide? I am going to file a complaint now. Watch me file a case under habeus corpus against the man.' His heavy body bounced with anger. The mere threat made amma and Aunt feel better. They sat up as though they had been injected with superpower.

'Uncle, she is not a minor. If you file a complaint now, how are they going to handle it? Moreover, they had a wedding at a mosque and had it registered.'

His glare landed on her like a sword, sending sparks flying. *How dare you, after all a woman, argue with me about this?* his eyes seemed to say.

'So, what do you propose – we just let it go? I will file a case against him for forcing her to change her religion as well.' His short stature and the way he wriggled when he spoke animatedly reminded her of a fish writhing on land.

The pride and force in his voice annoyed Anitha. With empty words that meant nothing, this retired bank manager with nothing else to do had taken it upon himself to bring the elopers to justice.

Just as he'd sworn, Nair filed a case under habeus corpus.

Anitha didn't think it made any sense. 'No one has kidnapped her. She has gone willingly. Why drag this to court?' she voiced her disagreement. He flung a bunch of newspapers in her face and they scattered. She bent down to pick them up. She identified them as the weekly *Kalakaumudi* and the daily *Janmabhoomi*. She was furious at him for flinging them at her but stopped herself from reacting and tried to decipher his intent instead.

'Open your eyes and read it, see what it says!' Nair's voice boomed menacingly. He stepped back and dropped in a chair, panting.

Anitha hastened to scan the newspapers. The middle of *Kalakaumudi* had a page folded down. She unfolded it and read the piece underlined in pen. It was an article that said that 180 girls had been enticed with love to forcefully convert to Islam as part of a strategy to mount an attack on Hinduism. They were terming this 'love jihad'. She put the newspaper away and picked up *Janmabhoomi*. There, she read that 2,864 girls had been converted to Islam in this way so far. Confused, she saw the date on the paper. 27 September 2009 on *Janmabhoomi* and 10 June 2012 on *Kalakaumudi*. She looked at him quizzically as if to ask what he was trying to say.

More than his determination to overcome the issue at hand, he seemed to be driven by the desire to stir up trouble and she wanted to distance herself from that despicable attitude. 'I'm going to leave, aunty. I can't stay here any longer,' she said quietly, which the Nair heard.

'You go. Who asked you to come, anyway? This is a matter of my family's reputation and protecting their honour is my responsibility. Coming here just to act righteous and trying to stop me from doing my duty is not right. It's best if everyone sticks to acting their age,' he said.

She went back home feeling rather rattled by how loud and forceful he sounded despite his age. She also realized that the news articles he had thrust upon her as the whole truth had left a mark on her mind.

The next day, after they registered their case and were preparing to meet with a lawyer, they received a call from the police. Krishnan Nair answered the call. 'Girija, apparently your daughter and son-in-law have presented themselves at the station as a married couple. Do you want to come with me and meet them there?'

His angry and ridiculing voice made Anitha panic. Not wanting to face him, she went out into the hall from an inner room. 'Oh god …!' Her aunt was sobbing loudly and shivering. Her amma was hugging her sister, trying to console her.

Everyone on their street was straining their ears to keep abreast of the happenings of their household. Anitha warned them about their surveillance. 'There is no need to create a scene. Stop crying, aunty,' she said and moved her to a sofa holding her by her arms. Her sobs became lengthy whimpers. Unable to express her own feelings on the matter, amma brought water and made her sister drink it.

Nair's anger and irritation erupted from deep within and the flesh on his face shook violently as he realized he had lost the battle. He was overtaken by a sort of panic. His grey eyebrow hairs pointed downwards from how high his furrowed brow reached. He stomped out saying he was going to bring the car around. Anitha noticed how his veshti flew up and down with a flourish, like a kite in the draught, from his hurried departure.

She did not know what was going to happen next and found herself feeling pushed into a corner. She felt as if the whole room was shaking to the rhythm of her aunt's gasps. Noticing her aunt's long hair flying in all directions because of the fan, Anitha walked over to the dining table in search of her handbag, pulled out a hair tie from inside it, gathered her aunt's hair and tied it back. Her heart broke at the sight of her crying. She began to believe that it was not going to be easy to pull her out of her grief.

It wouldn't be apt to say they walked her aunt to the car – they had to drag her. On their street with all houses sitting at comfortable distances from one another, a couple of heads could be spotted craning from behind the trees. 'Why have us endure such shame and humiliation, Krishna!' her mother mumbled under her breath. Her frail body shivered.

As the old Ambassador sped through the roads, Anitha breathed in the warm air gushing through the opened windows and pulled herself together. The three of them suffered quietly, feeling trapped not knowing what was going to happen at the police station. Because Nair's own intent was clear on what he was going to do when he got there, he drove the car measuredly. That half-hour drive felt like the most sorrowful journey of Anitha's life.

'It is my cruel fate that I have to set foot in such places. Oh god!' her aunt said as she stood in the verandah of the police station. Anitha glared at her and hissed, 'Aunty, please stay quiet.'

She tried in vain to make her conscious of the people working at the police station and the constables who were watching them. The policemen looked at them disdainfully. A pot-bellied policeman standing a little distance away from them pretended to leaf through his diary stealing glances at them every other second. His judgmental look made Anitha feel embarrassed. Being in that old building with its old chairs, dust-laden almirahs, disorganized stacks of newspapers, made her feel suffocated. 'Can I go outside and wait there for some time, sir?' she asked one of the officers hesitatingly.

'Please wait here, someone has gone to bring them over,' the sub-inspector replied sternly. He seemed to say, *what sort of irresponsible people are you?* Anitha ground her teeth.

She felt ashamed that she too was studying to someday be able to enjoy such authority. *Aren't we all humans first, titles and authority only after that?* Her frustration was building up. She slowly walked out into the verandah, sat her aunt down on a chair there and looked around for Krishnan.

She spotted him talking to an attorney under a tree. He looked furious. She was even more irritated at the sight of them. She went back into the office through the verandah. The police station writer looked up and saw her. Even though she noticed the indifference in his face, she pretended not to and tried to enter the inspector's office. The constable stopped her. His moustache was completely out of proportion with the rest of his physique. He had a large body and the belt trying to hold his cascading belly in place seemed to have failed trying.

'I want to talk to sir, please let me go in, sir.' Her fluent English prompted him to reconsider.

'Okay … please wait here, let me check with sir,' he said and passed through the wooden doors into the inspector's office. He re-emerged and said with annoyance, 'You can go in.'

Had the inspector declined her request, he would have expressed a different sort of annoyance at her. Such is human nature – especially people in authority. They were the worst, she thought as she opened the creaking wooden doors to the office. When the inspector looked up at her with apathy and said, 'Yes?' she just stood there, not knowing what to say next. He must have been around forty years old and had a brusque appearance.

'Sir, I am Anitha. The girl's sister. I am studying for the civil services exam in Thiruvananthapuram.' Her English seemed to impress him too.

'Yes, and?' he said.

'She has eloped unwittingly, sir. She needs to come back home with us somehow. Seeing her mother cry is unbearable. When they get here, could you please convince her to come home with us somehow, sir?' She tried to sound as desperate as she could, hoping that emphasizing and repeating the word 'somehow' would help convey the earnestness of her request.

The look he gave her in response seemed to ask her, *You call yourself an educated woman?*

'Do you or do you not know that the girl is a major? How can you expect me to send her home with you?' his voice had risen.

'About that—' she wanted to say more but sensed that she shouldn't, realizing he was right.

'Please go and sit outside. Some of my men have gone to bring them, we can talk once they get here.' His words struck her like a slap across her face. She realized there was no point in saying anything more and allowing herself to be humiliated any further and walked away quietly. Her face displayed her fatigue when she stepped out. She chided herself. *Did you speak like an educated woman? Was it right to speak to him this way? Begging him to send her home with you as if you were pleading before a village panchayat ...*

She was learning about checks and balances to protect civilian rights under Administrative Law and knew that subjecting someone to emotional duress was wrong.

Krishnan Nair walk into the inspector's office along with their lawyer.

When Kavya and Faisal arrived, Kavya stated that they were married, she had converted to Islam and was wearing the burqah by her own choice. Anitha stood frozen in silence as she quietly watched Kavya request permission to return with her husband and assert that she was ready to present herself at the court the following morning. Her aunt fell at her daughter's feet and cried profusely.

'Take the girl to the home and the boy will spend tonight at the station. Everyone else, please leave,' a policeman had instructed. As the scene unfolded in her mind – the couple following the policeman, coldly walking past their family as they stood and looked on helplessly – Anitha woke up with a start. The train was approaching Kozhikode.

Amma was waiting outside to greet her. The way she stood now, exactly like how she had stood against the compound wall of the police station, disheartened, led Anitha to believe that she had been standing there a long time waiting for her arrival.

'Tomorrow is the day of the verdict at the court. That's why we asked you to come.' Her amma spoke as she walked slowly. Both of them knew what the verdict was going to be.

'And what is that Krishnan Nair saying?' Anitha asked, grinding her teeth.

'Shh ...' amma gestured her to keep quiet. *He is here, inside the house.* That irritated her.

Her aunt was lying on the swing. She looked emaciated. Seeing Anitha walk in, she tried to get up eagerly. 'Lie back down calmly,' Anitha said, placing her hands on her shoulders and gently pushing her down. She then sat next to her.

Nair, who was busy scribbling something sitting at the table, looked up at her and then returned his attention to whatever he was doing, ignoring her. After Kavya had stated in front of the judge at the court during her previous visit that she was lawfully wedded to her husband, she had been permitted to leave with him. Later, Krishnan Nair had once again filed a case claiming that their wedding was invalid and that it was an act of love jihad, which was a punishable offence due to forceful conversion and marriage. They were awaiting verdict on that tomorrow.

'How are you, aunty, have you eaten?' Anitha asked her, running her fingers through her hair.

'Yes, I have eaten ... enough to remain alive,' her voice quavered.

'Don't say such things, aunty. Have you forgotten about the rest of us?' Anitha tried to cheer her up. A long silence ensued.

The morning rays of the sun bathed the garden, elevating their sense of a vast emptiness. She couldn't remember ever having to force herself this much to get out of bed. *What is the reason for this feeling*, she wondered, trying to calm herself down. She pulled out her cellphone to apprise Arun of the situation. She noticed she had received a message from Niloufer. She hesitated, not really wanting to read it as yet but eventually gave in. 'Don't you feel any guilt?' was all it said, which annoyed her. *Why should I feel any guilt?*

There could be many reasons people may fall in and out of love. Is it necessary for one to fall in love and then remain in love the same way for the rest of their lives? That sounded rather foolish. She pushed the thought aside and sent a 'good morning' to Arun. *It would have been nice to have him around at such a time*, she thought and that cheered her up.

Amma knocked on the door and entered her room. 'Oh, you're up? Okay, go shower and get dressed. After breakfast, we'll go to the court. They have asked us to come at eleven.'

Nair was busy working in the living room. Anitha had never liked his face and now she tried to avoid it as much as possible. That face that nothing could soften. He showed her such spite that she was sure he despised that she, being a woman, was consulted at all.

The three of them were sitting in a car outside the court. 'Is all this necessary? They've had a wedding and everything, then why the mess?' amma said, unable to hold it in anymore. Anitha, too, felt the same. *What else has this Nair done but make a mess?* She clenched her jaw and swallowed her anger. The expression on her aunt's face showed that she too was of the same mind as them but had been stuck in an awkward spot, unable to say anything openly.

This ends today. Whatever we need to do to keep her happy from now on, we will do that, Anitha planned. In a few weeks, she would be assigned her first posting. She felt a confidence that she could decide what to do next based on that. She would like to take her mother and her aunt away from this place where they didn't have to bother about the neighbours or this Nair.

'She has arrived. You can also get out of the car now,' they heard Nair and alighted from the car. Anitha tried to spot Kavya through her window. She saw her stepping out of the back of a black car. She was wearing a black purdah and a scarf around her head. Kavya's face radiated joy and hope. The girl she had seen grow up since her childhood without a shred of self-confidence, who lost her father at a young age and had spent her entire life growing weary yearning for love, was nowhere to be found.

Earlier, when the court had given Kavya the option to go back to her mother's house as part of its verdict on the love jihad case Nair had filed, she had refused vehemently. She had gone on to complete her graduation with the help of her friends and insisted on living in the campus hostel. Since that day, Anitha was seeing her only now.

All this began to make some sense to Anitha, she felt a great sense of relief wash over her. She said to her aunt, 'Let's not bother her anymore, as long as she is happy.' She and amma understood her meaning. Through her sunken eyes, her aunt watched her daughter intently from a distance.

Before Nair came back for them again, they got out of their car and walked towards the inner entrance of the court. *Kavya's husband Faisal must have already arrived.* Discerning that the perspiration on amma and her aunt's faces was not only because of the scorching heat, Anitha guided them indoors gently. In the small room with chairs arranged in rows, they approached the first row and sat down. The fan hanging from the high ceiling circulated the hot air around the room. Anitha noticed Nair talking to the attorney standing in a long verandah. Her gaze turned to the judge sitting in front of them.

She was a dark, hefty woman. The torrid heat from outside could be felt just as intensely indoors and her face was drenched in sweat despite the fan. Her eyes expressed her impatience to begin the proceedings. The attorneys from both sides were fully prepared and assumed their spots; the remaining rows of chairs were soon occupied by outsiders. Anitha's aunt buried her face into Amma's arm and cried softly.

'Shh … don't cry, please. The judge will get angry and send us out,' Anitha whispered into her ear. Her aunt's whimpering died down. Kavya and Faisal were brought in from two different rooms. Kavya was wearing the same purdah as before. Nair and his attorney argued why they felt the entire affair and marriage were acts of love jihad, their statements sounding more like the dialogues in a drama than logical viewpoints.

Anitha mentally counted the number of hearings they had appeared for by this point. *I hope this case comes to an end today after having dragged on for several months. At least then we can move forward and plan for what comes next.* Wondering whether she should be angry at Nair or her sister for the mess, her thoughts shifted to what a favourable verdict for them would even look like.

By the time the judge began delivering her verdict, the courtroom was overflowing with a passionate crowd, specifically mediapersons and members of local political parties. Their eagerness stemmed not only from a desire to know how the months-long trial would end but also from their curiosity about how the political spectacle would unfold. In her heart, she was worried how her mother and aunt were going to face the consequences of the case living in this town, where her family's reputation was being torn to shreds by the long-drawn legal battle.

Faisal appeared calm and composed. Anitha drew

strength from his demeanour and quiet confidence. It dawned on Anitha then that this is what true love looked like. His body language and Kavya's bold words bolstered her belief. *When the two of them have made a choice on their own to spend their lives with each other, no law or relative has any business questioning that.* She turned her gaze towards Kavya, who appeared completely aloof to her staring or the resentment in her eyes. 'I changed my religion by choice. I *chose* to get married to him. Please, just let us live in peace.' Kavya's stance has remained consistent and firm.

'No one in the name of law, society, religion or family can stop them from living together,' the judge finished reading out her verdict and Anitha's aunt started bawling. Anitha felt only relief – they were finally free. While the verdict was being read out, Anitha observed the happiness of Kavya – who had changed her name to Kathija after her wedding – and her aunt's earnest lament.

Nair's face had dejection written all over it. Dumbfounded with anger, he got up from his chair and stormed out of the courtroom. The three women remained fixed to their spots with lumps in their throats as they watched Kavya and her lawyer walk out, briefly looking in their direction before Faisal joined them.

The couple got into a black Scorpio.

Nair was bubbling with fury as he approached them. Anitha turned her face away from him. 'Did you see how she just walked away? Without a care in the world. Having birthed her and brought her up, it would have been better to just kill her off!' His voice was harsh. 'Okay, come, let's go. What's the point of standing here? Our honour has been destroyed; everything is destroyed,' he said, marching ahead of them. With teary eyes, amma held her younger sister's hand and Anitha held her by her shoulders and they led her to the car. They felt adrift, uncertain.

Kavya, who had got into her car with her husband, watched her mother walking in the sun through the window. Seeing tears rolling down her face, Faisal wrapped his arms around her shoulders and hugged her comfortingly. She had only just realized how the distance between her and her family had become impossible to bridge and the grief of having lost them choked her. Her heart ached as she wondered if she would ever get to see her amma, aunt and Anitha again. Unable to bear the sight of her mother's withered face and lifeless gait, she buried her face into her husband's chest and sobbed; Faisal embraced her tightly to comfort her. Her shaking body tried to find solace in his firm grasp, but failed.

The bloodlust in Nair's eyes frightened Kavya and Faisal. He worried if he might be forced into paying too big a price for their victory in the court. He waited for Nair to start his car and drive out of view before signalling his driver to start their car.

43

WHILE IMRAN GOT DRESSED FOR OFFICE, VINUTHA stood in his kitchen, cooking for him. Their relationship and shared affection felt light and effortless. The hesitation and inhibitions that Imran had felt earlier had now disappeared. In the last few months, Imran had begun to see life very differently thanks to his friendship with Vinutha.

He had begun to fully absorb what it meant to live for himself and the freedom that came with that. He had needed the time to accept that it wasn't a sin to live it up, as long as it did not harm anyone else. 'If someone doesn't like you back, you don't need to throw out everyone else associated with them from your life, silly. Who in this world is free from problems or worries? You can't let yourself change this way. Don't vent your frustration at me,' he was reminded of Niloufer's reproach over the phone from the other day.

'Breakfast is ready, come!' Vinutha's voice brought him back to the present. The table was full – there was bread-omelette, oatmeal and fruit juice.

'Why are you putting in so much effort?' he asked her.

'It's not really much effort. Sit down, let's eat.' As they began eating, she asked him, 'I'm going to a party after work. Do you want to come too?'

'Yes, but no drinking, okay?'

'No problem,' she said and laughed. He thought her sharp nose and dimpled cheek were adorable.

'Dei, what's with that look on your face? We've been living together for two months now. Why are you looking at me as if it's the first time you are seeing me?' she said, rapping him gently on his head with her knuckles.

'So what if I am? I'm enchanted by you every minute,' he replied, and they broke out into laughter.

He had trimmed his beard short, although it would grow back to its usual length by the time he went home. Then he wouldn't need to come up with any explanations for his attha. He had removed Anitha entirely from his mind and all he wanted was to be close to Vinutha; he felt contented with her in his life.

As they were driving to work, Vinutha was in high spirits and her joy was infectious. 'You said you'll come to the party, which is why I'm this happy,' she said and winked. Her laughter reverberated through the car and Imran's heart. Outside, it had begun drizzling lightly.

When Niloufer called Anitha on the phone, she was at a restaurant with Arun. 'What's new? How are you?' she asked.

'I'm fine. Arun and I have come out to eat. You tell me, how are you?'

'I'm also fine. Did you know Imran and Vinutha are now a thing?'

'Oh …?' Anitha said. Since she didn't really care, she had nothing more to say.

'Okay then, let's talk later.' Niloufer hung up, disappointed.

If Imran had changed into this person sometime back, would I still have left him? Anitha wondered. She couldn't simply ignore the hatred for Islam which had taken root in her heart. Choosing someone who fit in with her lifestyle and career made sense to her and she felt reassured that she had made the right decision.

'Where are you lost? What did your friend say?' Arun interrupted her chain of thought.

'Oh. Nothing much, she'd called just like that. Shall we order the main course?' she changed the topic and took a sip of water.

Arun looked dapper. A ranked officer in the police force, she found his stately appearance and charming manner of speaking very attractive. Within a few days of meeting him during their training, she had grown to like him but had not yet broken up with Imran. It had unsettled her to have been drawn to another man while she and Imran had still been in love. *If this is the case, have I unconsciously started growing distant from Imran?* she had wondered. From a pragmatic point of view, she justified her attraction to Arun as the opportunity to make her life simpler and live more freely.

'When you come to my village, you may need to wear a burqah, you shouldn't remove your headscarf. Only then will my attha and amma approve.' Imran's words flashed in her mind momentarily. She felt relieved and then a rush of elation at her narrow escape. She reached out with her right hand and grabbed Arun's left hand tightly as he sat across from her, scanning the menu. He looked at her and smiled and promptly turned his attention back to the menu.

'Anitha, you seem to be in a strange mood today. What's going on?' Arun finally asked, interrupting her daydreaming.

'Nothing at all,' she smiled sweetly at him. She noticed that the few people scattered about the restaurant were looking at them and whispering. Arun noticed this too and lowered his gaze, but Anitha didn't think it was worth worrying about and nonchalantly dug into her food.

She seems to be different today, unlike her usual self, Arun mused.

44

'HOW LONG ARE WE GOING TO KEEP LIVING LIKE THIS?'

Vinutha finally raised the question, prompting Imran to lift his gaze from his laptop and look at her. He seemed taken aback by the unexpectedness of her question.

'It's you I'm asking,' she clarified before placing the cup of tea in her hand on the table close by and sitting on the bed, facing him. 'I've already told my elder brother about us. My family would be willing to accept our match as well. Now it is you who has to decide and talk to your family.'

How simple she makes it all sound, he admired her clarity with astonishment and reflected into his own inability to do the same.

Vinutha is educated. Her entire family is well-educated and in prestigious jobs. He felt inadequate in the face of their broad-mindedness and progressive thinking. There was no way for him to compare her status with that of his own or his family's, or the environment he grew up in.

'Okay then … I'm going to go take a shower,' she said and left. He realized she must have noticed he had been caught off-guard by her question and she didn't want him to feel uncomfortable.

A few weeks earlier, when he had visited home, his attha had been getting ready to step out for collecting his payments. 'I'm not taking the driver. I want you to come with me,' he had said, to Imran's surprise.

Attha would never really ask him to come along in this way. 'Our poor child eats hotel food every day. He has taken leave especially to come home for four days. Give him some good homecooked meals,' he would usually say and insist that his son rest at home.

When attha asked him to join him that day, his amma rushed over. 'No, I won't allow this. My son has come home after two months; let him stay home and rest.'

Aabida kuppi also joined in. 'Don't you see the child has no flesh on his bones? A country hen from our grove is being prepared for him,' she said fondly.

'Wait two days to shower your love upon him. We absolutely need to go today. It would be best if Imran comes along,' Attha insisted gently.

Once they left, Imran chanted the dua before undertaking travel as usual without being prompted. He smiled at his mother and aunt who stood watching affectionately as they departed, and took their leave with a salaam.

'So where shall we go first?' he asked his father, waiting for directions.

'Pudukotai, then we go to Thirupathoor and then Karaikudi. We will cover three places today.'

He was bewildered. It had been a while since his attha had gone and collected dues himself. 'Why are you doing this yourself? Don't you have Ajeez, Sabeeq, Murugan from the store at your disposal?'

'That's not it, pa. We've started selling footwear recently. I wanted to have a walkaround, check on how well our products are being marketed, how the goods are moving. That's why.'

What he said made sense. He hadn't been home since they had set up the shoe mart. Attha had told him over the phone that the business was doing well. After the use of bicycles declined, so did the need for spare parts. Thankfully, he had been able to identify another area to set up a business in quickly and run it successfully. He was certainly a smart man. Imran was sure attha wished that he stayed and ran the business along with him. But attha himself had not brought that up to him even once.

'Son, I could never pursue higher studies. I want you to study, work at a reputed firm, become a manager, wear fancy suits and live well,' he would often say to him. 'I would be even prouder if you cleared IAS or IPS exams and became an officer. People of our community need to seek positions of authority, pa,' he would add.

His passion for that goal was evident in his voice; it was not merely a wishful thought.

'What's the point in having all this money? Or respect in one's village? We still remain answerable, even to a tahsildar, I have realized. Our community must acquire higher levels of authority, Attha.' Imran noticed that his voice carried a hint of regret, this time around. The day he had decided on his job, he had also decided to stop studying further. Even as attha had told him, 'You can keep working but also try to keep studying for the civil services on the side.'

When he came to know that his son was completely disinterested in doing so, Rasangam stopped bringing it up at all. But Imran knew the desire must still reside in some corner of his heart. The two of them waited to see who would be the one to shatter the silence that enveloped them; Imran drove on.

Attha was watching the passersby walking along the edges of the road. All these years later, he had still not stopped searching for his dear brother. Imran had asked him once, 'Do you think he is still alive?' He had replied, 'Usually, mentally unstable people don't die young unless they meet with an accident of some sort. That is what fuels my hope and prompts me to keep looking for him. I believe Allah will grant my dua.' It did not come as a surprise to Imran how strong attha's conviction and belief in the power of his dua was.

'How is chinnattha doing? Has he visited you recently? How are my sisters doing?' Imran wanted to change the topic because his attha would get very sad at the thought of Hanifa periattha. He wanted to distract him.

'No, he hasn't visited ... his focus is entirely on himself and his Tabligh Jamaat work as usual. He had called one day. Apparently, he has arranged for the nikkah of one of his daughters.'

'For that child?!' Imran was shocked. 'She is not even sixteen yet!'

'Yes, I also asked him why he wanted to marry her off at such a young age. To that, he simply said, "All that is okay." He decides what the rules are for the girls. He hasn't bothered to educate them. When I ask him, he shrugs it off saying they've got an Aalima degree from the madrasa. Madrasas are a dime a dozen around their village. Instead of sending the children to get formal education, he is sending them to earn Aalima degrees. That lunatic has not even allowed them to study till tenth class. We have not been blessed with a daughter but if we had been, I would have ensured she studied to become a doctor. Allah has given him six daughters ...' Attha's voice expressed his deep yearning. He had said the same thing many times before.

'If I had a daughter, I would have given her a very good education.' The words came straight from his heart.

'Shall I try talking to him? I was planning to go to their house next week when I have some time off work.. I'll see if I convince him to delay the marriage by a bit. Isn't it illegal as well?'

'To that madman? Is it even possible for anyone to talk sense into him? The man is utterly ignorant!'

This was the first time Imran had heard his father use such strong language. Frustrated at the inexplicable actions of his younger brother, Attha said wearily, 'Your mother has also started looking for a bride for you. Offer your dua, Allah is mighty. I wonder what is in our naseeb, *khayr* – may good fortune befall you.'

'For me? Why this early?' Imran wanted to ask but refrained.

They were travelling along narrow tar roads flanked by ponds on both sides. The water looked beautiful. 'We've had good rains this year,' Attha mumbled to himself and then said aloud, 'Do you know our Jawaad?'

'Who is that? I don't think so.'

'You know Rasaaq who works at our shop, right? Jawaad is his son. You may have met him as a child.'

So what? Imran waited for him to elaborate as he drove on quietly.

'He had gone to live in Mumbai, twenty years ago. There, he used to sell vegetables on a pushcart through the streets. He has reached a good place now. He has just bought a house, it seems. His children are studying in college,' he said and paused.

The fog in Imran's mind started clearing up a little. He had been wondering why his attha was talking so much about someone who lives in Mumbai. He realized he was setting the stage for something else he wanted to tell him.

'He has seen you around, now and again. He mentioned it when he was visiting his family last week.

This life is not permanent, you know; it offers us an opportunity to collect goodness for our *aagirathi*, our afterlife. We come here as mere visitors. We can't simply live in this materialistic world and leave on our own terms. We are obligated to answer to God for every action of ours in the afterlife. It wouldn't be wise to pawn one's afterlife for the pleasures of this transient existence.'

'Oh ...' Imran's voice sank, understanding his meaning. He didn't know what to say. Attha's attention returned to the ponds and trees around them.

Attha doesn't usually talk much. He wouldn't probe any further, Imran knew, and drove on silently.

Until they had reached home the next day, a heavy silence had fallen over the two of them, which Imran knew better than to ignore.

'A penny for your thoughts, sir?' Vinutha said as she dried her hair with a dryer.

When did she finish her shower? Did I not even notice? he wondered.

'Oh, it's nothing. Just like that, dear,' he said aloud.

She chuckled without making a sound and blinked at him. The laughter was a ruse to return him to his usual self. He knew well that she didn't want to upset him even for a second and took care to cater to him all the time.

'What did I say that made you retreat into your shell like this? Please relax.'

'Nothing, really. I was just thinking about how to tell people at home about what you said. Just feeling a little muddled, that's all.'

Vinutha sat next to him and placed her head on his shoulder. 'No rush, you do as you wish and take your time. But I can't live without you; just remember that.'

They were both deeply emotionally invested. A war raged within Imran. He knew his attha wouldn't assent to the match until Vinutha converted to Islam. How he was going to tell Vinutha that, he did not know.

When they first started growing closer to each other, he was in a crisis and under tremendous stress. He had needed her love and intimacy to tide him over. Nothing else had seemed important then. He knew he couldn't live without her either. But what he couldn't figure out was how to set about making it happen.

Even though he did not personally agree with the Qur'an's stance on how getting married to or having a relationship with women of other religions amounted to adultery, he couldn't help but wonder how he could get his family to accept his choice; how would his attha take it? His head felt like it would explode worrying about all this. But what could he do to get to the bottom of his complicated situation?

Maybe, talking to Niloufer and Dhanasekar might help get clarity. He decided he and Vinutha would go to Chennai.

45

VINUTHA UNDERSTOOD THE REASON IMRAN WAS IN turmoil. Yet, she pretended to be indifferent to it. She figured that what hadn't been a problem in his and Anitha's case had now grown to be a problem in Imran's mind when it came to their relationship. She did not, however, want to concern herself with her role in the problem.

She fully understood his situation. She also hadn't been able to come up with any great ideas about what she could do to help the pieces fall in place. She sat at the dressing table and began combing her hair.

Her elder brother had been asking her about how things were going for a couple of days now. She didn't know what to tell him. He had been living in California for so long, he seemed to have forgotten all about how things happened in India. Festivals and religions had lost all significance for him. He was married to a white woman and Vinutha could not expect him to grasp Imran's situation or confusion. She decided she would talk to her father and have him explain the situation to her brother.

She knew it was religion that was the issue. She didn't think he would insist on such a precondition. She understood him very well, but she wished he would rid himself of this excessive brooding over how best to handle this situation.

The Chennai heat struck her face and scorched her. 'I only think of the heat whenever I think of Chennai, it's horrible …' Vinutha grumbled to Niloufer.

Imran knew she was not the type to fuss over such trivial things. He worried about what Niloufer might think of her. The heat was still bearable. When Dhanasekar pulled up at the pick-up point, they got into the car and drove out of the airport.

'The flight arrived on time, didn't it, Dhanasekar.' Imran started talking for the sake of dispelling the silence.

'Yes, Imran,' Dhana replied. Vinutha smiled in agreement.

'Are you planning to head back today itself?' Niloufer asked Imran.

'Pch … I haven't decided as yet. I might go home from here and maybe Vinu could return by herself. And how is your daughter doing?' Imran asked.

'She's living it up,' Niloufer said and smiled, looking at Vinutha. She smiled faintly in response. Perhaps it was Vinutha's demeanour, highly fashionable attire and undeniable beauty that did not allow the two women to gel.

She looks far more beautiful and fashionable than Anitha. Niloufer remembered Imran mentioning that she came from a very wealthy family. She nursed a faint doubt that her money made her haughty.

Dhana was driving towards Park Hotel.

'Where are you going?' Imran asked.

'The Park,' he replied.

'No need. Just take us to some restaurant that won't be too crowded or loud.'

'Okay.' He turned onto Khader Nawaz Khan Road.

Since it was noon, the restaurant they chose was not crowded. There were one or two couples sitting a few tables apart. A Nepalese waiter greeted them and ushered them in, asked if they had made a reservation. Niloufer replied that they hadn't.

'Okay,' he said and led them to a table close by.

'I'm going to wash my hands,' Vinutha said and looked at Niloufer to check if she wanted to join her.

'Sure,' Niloufer said and went along with her. 'I'm so happy to finally meet you. Imran has told us so much about you. He said you're a very sweet person and have been a huge support for him while he was going through the whole Anitha debacle.'

Vinutha hugged Niloufer tightly and thanked her. Niloufer had not expected the hug and felt her heart melt.

When the two of them returned to the table, Dhana noticed a calmness spread across Niloufer's face. He looked at both of them closely, trying to figure out if Niloufer's reservations about Vinutha had been put to rest. Imran told them that they had already ordered what they wanted and pushed the menu towards the two women so they could place theirs.

When Vinutha ordered a glass of wine with her food, Niloufer pretended not to notice.

'So what have you decided then, Imran? You *are* going to talk to your family, aren't you?' No one expected Niloufer to get directly to the point. Imran sat buried under the weight of his own mind.

Dhana picked up the glass of water sitting in front of him, took a sip from it and set it back down.

'Nilo, please don't rush this. Let's talk through it slowly. He's already in a lot of confusion.' Vinutha placed her hand on Niloufer's shoulder and smiled.

Their food arrived and they started eating.

'You don't know how to break this news to your family and get their blessings, right? Anitha's situation was different. Talking about it at home and getting permission would have not been as much of an issue,' Niloufer spoke softly.

'Keep quiet, Nilo,' Imran said, taking a break from eating his pasta. It pained Vinutha to see him like that. Niloufer fell quiet.

Dhana asked, 'What will they say to oppose this? That

she is a Hindu girl? Will they be okay if she converts to Islam?'

Niloufer replied, 'They will want her to convert to Islam.'

Dhana grew quiet. Imran should be the one to provide the answers from then on.

'I don't have any objections to that. I'm ready to convert to Islam. I can't stand to see Imran in such pain,' Vinutha chimed in.

'Then what's the issue!' Niloufer's widened eyes sparkled.

'No, Vinu,' Imran said, immediately overruling her. 'I can't ask you or push you to make such a huge change. Isn't it your right to choose?' He struggled to internalize that they had so swiftly arrived at a solution to such a complex problem.

In the meantime, their food grew cold.

46

IMRAN GOT ON THE TRAIN, SPREAD OUT HER BEDDING and placed her suitcase carefully under her berth. He kept a water bottle on the ledge by the head of her berth. 'Take care. Call me when you reach. I'll also have reached home by then,' he said.

Vinutha nodded, quietly basking in his care. Dhana stood outside the train. The time of departure was getting closer. Imran got off the train and stood next to Dhana. The horn blared, announcing the departure of the train as it slowly started moving. Vinutha waved and Imran waved back at her.

Dhana patted his shoulder and said, 'Come, you have to catch your bus at Koyambedu.' They started walking. Until Imran had boarded his bus, neither of the men spoke. Dhana handed him a bottle of water and hugged him. 'Okay, you better get on the bus now. They are getting ready to leave,' he said.

'Imran ... be careful with your attha, da,' he added as his eyes welled up.

Unable to respond to him, Imran simply swallowed the lump in his throat. He got on the bus, sat in his seat, looked at his friend through the window and waved.

The bus set off on its journey.